DATE DUE

THREE NOVELS

Nina Berberova

THREE NOVELS

The Resurrection of Mozart
The Waiter and the Slut
Astashev in Paris

Translated from the Russian by
Marian Schwartz

Chatto & Windus
LONDON

Published in 1990 by
Chatto & Windus Ltd
20 Vauxhall Bridge Road
London SW1V 2SA

A CIP catalogue record for this book is available
from the British Library

ISBN 0 7011 3608 1

Copyright © Actes Sud 1989, 1986, 1988
Translations copyright © Marian Schwartz 1990

Typeset by The Spartan Press Ltd
Lymington, Hants

Printed and bound in Great Britain by
Butler & Tanner Ltd, Frome and London

CONTENTS

———— ❦ ————

The Resurrection of Mozart

I

In the early days of June 1940, just at the time when the French army was beginning its final and irrevocable retreat after the breach at Sedan, on a quiet warm evening, a group of four women and five men were sitting in a garden under the trees, about thirty miles from Paris. They were in fact talking about Sedan, talking of how the last few days had restored to that name which, like crinoline, had long since gone out of fashion, the ominous connotations it had had before; this town, which none of them had ever seen, and which had died in the time of their grandfathers, seemed to have been resurrected in order to relive the tragic events that were destined for it alone.

The silence was so complete that when they stopped talking and returned to their own private thoughts, they could hear through the open windows the clock ticking in the large old house. The sky was green, clear and lovely, and the stars were just beginning to shine, so few and far-flung that they failed to form any definite pattern. The old trees – acacias, limes – neither breathed nor trembled, as if standing stock-still were a safeguard against something that was invisible to men but somehow immanent in the summer evening. The hosts and their guests had just finished supper; the table had not yet been cleared. Some wine-glasses were still on the table. Slowly, the green light of the darkening sky transformed the faces of the seated company which was now obscured by shadows. They were talking about war and about the omens of war. A young woman, a guest who had driven out from town with her husband and sister, restraining her brassy voice, remarked that she had seen a meteor a fortnight before.

'It was about this time of day. The sky was just as hazy. At first it looked like a falling star, but it was so long and it was so bright.'

'You probably wouldn't even have noticed it a year ago,' said another guest, smiling. This was Chabarov, a bald, robust man with a drooping black moustache and wearing a bright blue shirt. He was a groundsman at a château about eight miles away and had just arrived on his bicycle.

'A year ago,' said Vassily Georgievich Sushkov, the host, a tall man, taller than anyone else at the table, grey-haired but not yet old, with a sharp and furtive look in his eye. 'Yes, it was exactly a year ago today that Nevelsky died. He knew a lot of this was coming. He predicted so much of it.'

'Well, he couldn't have picked a better time to die. At least he doesn't have to see what we see. If he were resurrected he'd either spit in disgust or break down and cry.'

Facing the hostess, at the opposite end of the table, sat a Frenchman brought along by Chabarov but whom no one else really knew. Simply, and without any fussy apology, he asked them to translate what they were all saying.

'Monsieur Daunou, we were talking about the dead, and what they would say if they were resurrected and saw what's going on now,' replied Maria Leonidovna Sushkova.

Daunou took his black pipe out of his mouth, furrowed his brow, and smiled.

'Is it worth waking the dead?' he said, looking his hostess straight in the eye. 'I suppose I might well invite Napoleon to come and have a look at our times, but I'd certainly spare my parents the pleasure.'

Suddenly everyone started talking at once.

'Resurrect them for your sake or for theirs? I don't understand,' Manyura Krein, who had come from Paris, asked with a lively expression, not addressing anyone in particular and no longer trying to conceal her loud voice. She had a full mouth of her very own white teeth, which gave the impression of being false. 'If it were for their sake, then of course you'd resurrect Napoleon and Bismarck and Queen Victoria, and maybe even Julius Caesar. But if I could bring someone from the past back to life for my sake, just for mine, then that's an entirely different thing. That calls for some thought. Such a large choice, so many temptations . . . still, silly as it sounds, I think I'd resurrect Pushkin.'

'A charming, fun-loving, marvellous man,' said Maria Leonidovna Sushkova. 'What a joy it would be to see him alive.'

'Or maybe Taglioni?' continued Manyura Krein. 'I'd lock her up at home so I could look at her whenever I wanted.'

'And then take her to America,' put in Chabarov, 'and let the impresarios tear her to shreds.'

'Come on, if you're going to resurrect anyone, then don't resurrect Taglioni,' said Fyodor Egorovich Krein with barely repressed irritation. He was Manyura's husband, twice her age, and a friend of Sushkov's. 'There's no need to be frivolous. I would make the best of the occasion. I would drag Tolstoy back into God's world. Wasn't it you, dear sir, who denied the role of the individual in history? You who declared that there would be no more wars? And wasn't it you who took a sceptical view of vaccination? No, don't try to wriggle out of it now. Just have a look at the result.' It was evident that Fyodor Egorovich had scores to settle with Tolstoy and that he had an entire text prepared should they happen to meet in the next life.

'*Avec Taglioni on pourrait faire fortune*,' Chabarov repeated his thought in French.

'And I, gentlemen,' piped in Sushkov's mother, who wore heavy violet powder and reeked of some unpleasant perfume, 'and I, gentlemen, would resurrect Uncle Lyosha. Wouldn't he be surprised?'

No one knew who Uncle Lyosha was, so no one said anything for a minute or two. Little by little the conversation had drawn everyone in, taking them far from that evening, that garden and into the past, the recent or the very distant past, as if someone had already made a firm promise to wave a magic wand and fulfil everyone's wish, so that now the only problem was in making a choice, and it was a difficult choice because no one wanted to miscalculate, especially the women.

'No one but Mozart will do for me, though. Yes, it has to be Mozart,' Maria Leonidovna thought to herself. 'There's no one else I want, and it would be useless anyway.'

She had decided not out of any morbid love of music, as can happen with women who have reached a certain age and who are generally thought of as 'cultured', but merely because she connected that name in her mind with her earliest childhood, and because it lived on as something pure, transparent, and eternal that might take the place of happiness. Maria Leonidovna smoked avidly and waited for someone else to say something. She didn't feel like talking herself. It was Magdalena, Manyura Krein's sister, a young woman of thirty, full-figured and pale, with unusually rounded shoulders, who spoke up. The sight of her always brought to mind those undeniable statistics about how in Europe so many millions of young women had been left single because there weren't enough husbands to go round.

'No, I wouldn't resurrect a single famous man,' said Magdalena, with a certain disdain for men of renown. 'I'd much prefer an ordinary mortal. An idealistic youth from the early nineteenth century, a follower of Hegel, a reader of Schiller; or a courtier to one of the French kings.'

She shrugged her heavy shoulders and looked around. But already it was nearly dark, and one could barely make out the faces round the table. But the stars were now quite visible overhead, and the sky seemed familiar again.

Chabarov didn't say anything for a long while. Finally he made a muffled nasal sound, drummed his fingers on the table, opened his mouth, but suddenly hesitated, said nothing, and sank back into his thoughts.

The ninth person present, who had been silent until then, was Kiryusha, Sushkov's nineteen-year-old son and Maria Leonidovna's stepson. In the family he was considered a little backward. Slowly he unglued his thick, wide lips and, gazing trustfully at his stepmother with his blue and very round eyes, asked if it were possible to resurrect two people at the same time.

God alone knows what was going through his dreamy mind at that point. He seemed to think that everything had already been de-

7

cided by the others and that only the details remained to be settled.

'*Mais c'est un vrai petit jeu,*' noted Daunou with a sad laugh, and immediately everyone seemed to move and smile once more, as if returning from far away. 'Everyone has their own private passion, and everyone is being terribly serious about it.'

Maria Leonidovna just nodded at him. 'Mozart, of course, only Mozart will do,' she repeated to herself. 'And it's a good thing I'm not young any more and don't have any physical interest in seeing him. We could sit up till dawn, and he could play our piano and we'd talk. And everyone would come to see him and listen to him – the neighbours' gardener and his wife, the postman, the shopkeeper and his family, the station master . . . What a joy it would be! And tomorrow there'd be no post, no trains, nothing at all. Everything would be topsy-turvy. And there wouldn't be any war. No, there would be war all the same.'

She lit another cigarette. For a moment the match illuminated her thin, slightly worn face and her delicate, beautiful hands. Everything about her, except her face, was feminine, youthful and sleek, particularly her light and silent walk. Everyone noticed when

Maria Leonidovna suddenly got up and walked out under the trees, and then came back to the table, and they could see the lit end of her cigarette in the darkness of the advancing night.

A chill came up about then from the low-lying part of the garden, where two little stone bridges crossed the narrow loops of the flower-banked stream. Old Mrs Sushkova, wrapped in a shawl, was dozing in her chair. Kiryusha was looking up blankly, and it was clear that like the trees and stars he was merely existing and not thinking. And suddenly, somewhere far off, perhaps twenty-five or thirty miles away to the east, where the sun rises in the summer, the sound of gunfire rumbled, burst out, and then disappeared. It was very much like thunder and yet completely different.

'Time we were on our way,' everyone started saying immediately, and Manyura Krein, jangling her bracelets, ran into the house for her coat and bag.

They went through the dining room and big dark hallway and came out into the yard where the car was parked. Sushkov's mother was going back to Paris as well. She put on a hat with a big violet-coloured flower; even her suitcase was a shade of violet. The motor

9

idled a few moments, and then, cautiously spreading its black wings, the car backed up to the gates. Krein, sitting behind the steering wheel, waved once again to those left behind. Manyura, whose porcelain mouth alone was illuminated, smiled behind the glass and said something. The car started up, stopped, shifted into forward, and as if it had hauled itself out, disappeared, leaving behind it a wake of invisible, acrid exhaust.

Chabarov went to find the bicycles.

'We'd be very happy to see you here any time,' Sushkov told the Frenchman. 'We're staying all summer, and on Sundays, as you see, our friends visit. You're always welcome.'

'*Enchanté, monsieur*,' Daunou replied. 'I have spent an unforgettable evening.'

And following behind Chabarov he kissed Maria Leonidovna's hand.

The next day, as usual, Vassily Georgievich took the train into town, leaving Maria Leonidovna and Kiryusha to themselves. That Monday, at one o'clock in the afternoon, several dozen aeroplanes bombed Paris for the first time.

II

News of the bombardment of Paris only came that evening. During the day you could hear the gunfire, but it was so far away that you couldn't tell whether it was in Paris or Pontoise, where it had been a few days before. In the evening the papers arrived, and all the people who lived in the little village, in the centre of which stood a neglected church with a caved-in roof, came spilling out into the modest avenue of sturdy plane trees that led from the café to the *mairie*.

The village consisted almost entirely of old women. Of course they may have only been, as in any French village, about half the population, but they were the ones you saw most often. Seeing them out in the street, talking together or shopping or shaking out a rag or hanging out clothes, they seemed to make up nine-tenths of the inhabitants.

Some of them were no more than fifty, and they were still smart and cheerful, just turning grey, rosy-cheeked and sharp-eyed. Others were wrinkled and toothless, with swollen veins. Others, who could remember the invasion of the Germans in 1870, were hunched up and barely able to put one sore foot in front of the other, and they had darkened hands, long black nails, and lifeless faces. They were all much of a kind, talking to each other in the same way, and using the same words, wherever they met, be it on street corners, beneath the plane trees, or by their front gates. They all wore wide calico aprons that either tied at the back or buttoned in front. Some wore steel glasses on their noses and knitted, rocking in a chair and holding the skein of wool under their left arms. Almost all of them were widows of men killed in the last war, and all without exception had seen either a son or a son-in-law set off for this war.

That evening, in the shady lane that ran alongside the fence to the Sushkovs' garden, the silence was broken. Kiryusha came to tell Maria Leonidovna that Paris had been bombed, buildings destroyed, warehouses burned, and more than a thousand killed or wounded. Maria Leonidovna looked at Kiryusha, who was smiling broadly, and it saddened her that this human being, who was now completely grown, was still the same child she had first met twelve years before. There was a time – and lately she had thought of it often – when he had suddenly decided to learn the alphabet. A brief light had pierced the darkness of that sick brain. He had tried to learn the letters, but nothing ever came of it. It had all ended with Kiryusha's short and relatively happy affair with the girl who worked in the charcuterie. Relatively happy because after that he had started to get gradually worse.

Maria Leonidovna went through Paris in her mind. In that city, above all, was Vassily Georgievich, as well as their pretty, sunny, quiet apartment, which she loved so much. Then there were the Kreins, the Abramovs, the Snezhinskys, Edouard Zontag, Semyon Isaakovich Freiberg, Lenochka Mikhailova, and many many more who could have been wounded or killed. And when she thought about all those people living at various ends of the city, scattered across the old creased map of Paris that she kept in her mind, a flashing light lit up, here and there, and then went out.

'Yes. This had to happen,' she told herself. 'We were talking about it only yesterday. So why did he go? The Kreins could have stayed on, too. Yesterday we said . . . What else were we talking about yesterday? Oh, yes! "You are God, Mozart, and of that fact yourself innocent." One ought to aspire to something that combines everything beautiful, pure and eternal, like those clouds, not all these terrible things, all these murders and lies. Before the ultimate silence closes in on you, shouldn't you listen to what the stars are saying to each other?'

She went over to the little radio, brand new, which Kiryusha was strictly forbidden to go near, and turned the knob. First a French voice spoke, then an English voice, then a German voice. All of it was crammed into that wooden box, separated only by invisible barriers. The voices all said the same thing. And suddenly it switched to music, singing, Spanish or maybe Italian, the voluptuous and carefree strumming of a guitar. But she picked up the word *amore*, and she turned the machine off and walked to the window, from which she could see the village road among the thick fields of oats, green and ash-grey.

On Tuesday, Wednesday and Thursday, soldiers were billeted on the village: heavy green trucks camouflaged with foliage as if decked out for a carnival and bearing numbers written in red lead paint brought in five hundred young, healthy, raucous soldiers and four officers wearing long overcoats and with tired, worried, feverish faces. A billeting officer appeared at Maria Leonidovna's door – the house the Sushkovs rented was by far the best in the village – and she immediately moved Kiryusha into the dining room, giving his room to the captain and the space in the annexe to three sub-lieutenants.

The four officers slept in their clothes. The sentry – sometimes a short, swarthy and yellow-eyed man or else a tall, erect and big-faced one – came to wake them several times during the night. Vassily Georgievich called every day; his call came to the post office at the corner of their side street and the square. A little boy missing his front teeth ran to fetch Maria Leonidovna, and she ran after him in her silent, girlish way, wearing whatever she happened to have on, ran into the tiny single-windowed building, picked up the receiver, and listened to Vassily Georgievich say that everything was fine, that he had received the money, seen Edouard, was eating with the Snezhinskys, would arrive on Saturday.

'I have soldiers staying with me,' she said, still out of breath from running. 'I've given them Kiryusha's room. And the annexe.'

'Maybe I should come? You're not afraid?'
'Why should I be afraid? Goodbye.'

And in fact, at that minute, she thought that she wasn't afraid in the least. In a way, it was even reassuring to have these polite, laconic men close at hand.

But at night she barely slept. She listened. From far away, in the dead of night, she caught the diffuse, persistent sound of a motorcycle. While the sound was on the far side of the woods, it was no more than a whisper, but as it got nearer it became louder and more focused, and then suddenly it was zooming down the lane and stopping at the house next door, where the sentry was posted. The motor was switched off, and then she could hear voices, steps. The gate banged. Someone was walking into the house, into her house, some stranger, and the old blind dog got up from its straw and went to sniff at his tracks in the gravel of the yard, growling. A light went on somewhere, she heard someone running through the house, through the annexe. Something clinked, a door slammed. Kiryusha was asleep close by, in the dining room, whose door she left open. These night sounds didn't frighten her any more. What frightened her was everything that was going on in the world that night.

She wasn't afraid of the quiet strangers either. They left the third night, leaving the doors and the gate wide open, leaving the village in trucks camouflaged with fresh branches. She wasn't afraid of the sentries who came to see them or of the five hundred strong, half-sober soldiers quartered all over the village. She was afraid of the air, the warm June air, through which gunfire rolled across the horizon and submerged her, her house, and her garden, along with the summer clouds. And there was no question that this puff of wind, which was somehow just like time itself, would in the end bring something terrible and ruinous, such as death itself. Just as, looking at the calendar, no one doubted any longer that in five, ten or fifteen days something dreadful was going to happen, so, feeling that faint breeze on her face day and night, she could say with assurance that it would bring to these parts murder, occupation, devastation and darkness.

For the air, over the last few days, had been warm, clear and fragrant. Kiryusha worked in the garden, watering the flowers in front of the house every evening and looking after the neighbours' ducklings. Maria Leonidovna, wearing a bright cotton print dress, and a scarf around her head, went to clean out the annexe, where she found a bag of cartridges which had been left behind and two unsealed letters, which she threw away without reading. There were cigarette butts in the cup by the washstand, and a charred newspaper lay on the floor. She made up Kiryusha's bed in his room and when the woman from next door came over to do the housework, told her to wash all the floors in the house.

On the same day, towards evening, fugitives from Soissons arrived at the neighbours': two fat, pale women, an old man, and some children. A mattress was laid out on the roof of their filthy car, and to the amazed questioning of the villagers the new arrivals explained that this was what everybody was doing now, that this was what would protect you from bullets. The old man was carried into the house by his hands and feet: he was unconscious.

Before night other fugitives arrived to stay in the sky-blue, toy-like house opposite the church. People said that some of the soldiers were still there, and were spending the night at the other end of the village. There seemed to be a stranger who had come from far away by foot or by car hiding in every house for the night. There were no lights, all was dark, but voices could be heard everywhere from behind the shutters; the café was full of shouting and singing. Under the plane trees the old ladies, who had stayed longer than was normal, spoke in low voices.

Maria Leonidovna locked the front door, hung the curtains over the windows, cleared away the remains of supper, and as she always did, sat in the next room and talked with Kiryusha while he got ready for bed. From time to time he exclaimed happily:

'I cleaned my teeth! I took off my left shoe!'

And if you didn't know it was a nineteen-year-old man in there – who ate enormous meals, snored loudly in his sleep, and couldn't read – you would think it was a ten-year-old boy going to bed and, for a joke, talking in a bass voice.

After she had turned out the light in the dining room and Kiryusha's room and went to her own, she stood for a long time by the open window and looked out at where, in the daytime, she could see the road and the oat-fields. Tomorrow Vassily Georgievich was due to return. The idea was pleasant and consoling. But today Maria Leonidovna had barely given a thought to her husband; in fact she hadn't stopped thinking about Mozart.

Or rather, not about Mozart himself.

Right now, as a new crescent moon appeared on the edge of this anxious but subdued night, her thoughts took on a special clarity. All day long, or rather, over the last few days and this evening, she had been asking herself the same question, and there was no answer to it: why was it that horror, cruelty, and affliction made themselves felt so easily, became concrete and weighed all the more heavily, whereas everything sublime, gentle, unexpected and full of charm cast a frail shadow across the heart and thoughts, so one couldn't touch it or look at it closely or feel its shape and weight? 'Except for love, of course,' she thought, standing by the window. 'Only love gives that kind of joy. But what about someone who doesn't want to love any more, who can no longer love? I have no one to love; it's too late for me. I have a husband, I don't need anyone else.'

And all of a sudden she thought she heard the latch on the gate click, and she distinctly heard someone come into the yard, take two steps, and stop.

'Who's there?' she asked quietly.

The darkness was not yet total, and the faint, blurred shadow of a man lay on the whitish gravel in the yard. The shadow moved and the gravel crunched. The man must have been able to see Maria Leonidovna clearly as she stood in the open window, to the right of the front door. The door, as Maria Leonidovna recalled, was locked. But the man, who was slowly and purposefully walking across the yard, made no response. She could hardly see him. He walked up the porch stairs, stopped three paces away from Maria Leonidovna, put out his hand, and the door opened. And when he had already walked into the house she wanted to scream. But, as in a dream, she was unable to produce any sound.

He was pale and thin, with a long nose and tangled hair. Everything he had on, from his boots to his hat, seemed to have been borrowed from someone else. His dusty hands were so slender and frail that he couldn't have used them even if he had wanted to. His face was weary, youthful, but it wasn't a boy's face. She could tell that he looked younger than he was, but that in fact he could be over thirty.

'Forgive me for frightening you,' he said in French, but with a slight foreign accent. 'Could I spend the night here somewhere?'

By the light of the lamp illuminating the spacious entryway Maria Leonidovna looked at him, standing silently and barely able to control herself. But the moment he uttered those first words and looked at her with his long, hesitant look, her fear passed, and she asked:

'Who are you?'

But he dropped his eyes.

'Where are you from?'

He shivered slightly, and his fingers clutched the upturned collar of his ample jacket, which might have been covering an otherwise naked body.

'Oh, from far, far away . . . and I'm so tired. I'd like to lie down somewhere, if that's all right.'

'A fugitive,' she decided, 'and maybe he's a Frenchman from some out-of-the-way province. Judging by his age, he could be a soldier; by his clothes, a fugitive? Maybe a spy?'

She led him to the annexe, thinking all the time that he might strike her from behind, but at the same time knowing he wouldn't. By the time they had entered the bedroom, she had lost all fear of him. He didn't even look around, but silently walked over to the bed, sat down on it, and closed his eyes. Between his shoe and trouser-leg she saw a thin, bare ankle.

'Do you want to eat?' she asked, closing the shutters on the low, folding windows from inside. 'It's the war, we're not supposed to show any light on the outside.'

'What did you say?' he asked, shuddering a little.

'I asked whether you'd like to eat something.'

'No, thank you. I had a bite to eat in your local restaurant. They were all full up, though, and couldn't give me a place to stay.'

She realised it was time she went.

'Are you alone?' she spoke again, rearranging something on the table as she passed.

'What do you mean "alone"?'

'I mean, did you come here – to the village – with friends or what?'

He raised his eyes.

'I came alone, just as I am, without any luggage,' he said smiling, but not revealing his teeth. 'And I'm not a soldier, I'm a civilian. A musician.'

She took another look at his hands, said goodnight, and having shown him where to turn off the light, walked out of the room.

That time she gave two turns to the lock in the door and suddenly, feeling a strangely animal weariness, went straight to bed and fell asleep. In the morning, as always, she got up early. Kiryusha was already in the garden bawling out some song, and in the annexe all was quiet.

III

Just before lunch she wondered, anxiously, if something had happened: the shutters and door were still closed. 'Can he still be asleep?' she thought. At four o'clock Vassily Georgievich was due to arrive, and a little before then she went again to see whether her lodger was up. She half-opened the door to the tiny entryway, and then the door of the room. The man was sleeping, breathing evenly. He had not removed any of his clothes, not even his boots. He lay on his back on the wide mattress, the pillow on one side. Maria Leonidovna closed the door again.

Vassily Georgievich was late getting back; the train coming from Paris had stopped for a long time at some bridge. Sushkov had carried a large suitcase from the station to the house, practically a trunk, on his broad, strong shoulder. It was full of things gathered up from their Paris apartment without which Vassily Georgievich could not imagine either his own or his wife's existence. There were his winter coat, Maria's old squirrel coat, warm underwear which he always wore during the winter, an album of photographs of Prague (he had lived in Czechoslovakia for a long time), expensive binoculars in their case, a pound of dried figs, which he liked to keep in reserve, a handsomely bound edition of Montesquieu's *Lettres Persanes*, and Maria Leonidovna's ball gown, sewn for a charity ball the year before at which she had sold champagne. Maria Leonidovna was surprised to see warm underwear and heavy coats in June. But Sushkov assured her that they might be cut off from Paris or could be forced to escape, and then they wouldn't know what was going to happen.

'Escape from here? Yes, of course, we'll have to escape if everyone else does. Those fugitives from Soissons are packing up their things again, and the old man is being carried out of the house to the car.' She took up the newspaper her husband had brought but learned nothing from it. Vassily Georgievich spoke to her sensibly and gently. Sometimes he argued with himself, sometimes he told her what Snezhinsky and Freiberg thought about what was going on. And everything he said was accurate, fair, intelligent.

'So, your officers have gone, have they?' he asked her. 'It must have been worrying for you.'

'They're gone, but since yesterday there's been a' – she wanted to say 'chap' but couldn't – 'man sleeping, staying in the annexe. He's still asleep. He must have come the seventy-five miles on foot.'

'My God, you've been staying here alone with my idiot and you're not afraid to let in strangers,' he exclaimed, never mincing words when it concerned Kiryusha. And catching her hand, scratching himself on her sharp nails, he kissed it several times.

Towards the end of the day Kiryusha told them in his incoherent way that the man staying in the annexe had gone. An hour later Maria Leonidovna heard him return and lock himself in again.

'That man came back. He must be sleeping again. Don't you go bothering him,' she told Kiryusha.

All the next day was the same: the visitor either lay or sat by the window and neither moved nor spoke. It was as if he were waiting for something. Or else he walked to the village for a little while, walked down the lane, across the square, down the avenue of plane trees, bought himself something to eat, and came back quietly.

Strange thoughts occurred to Maria Leonidovna. Sometimes she thought that the man was bound to be arrested. Why hadn't he told her his name? Why was he wearing clothes that didn't belong to him? If he wasn't a spy, then he was a deserter. Maybe he was Russian? In many years of living abroad, Maria Leonidovna had grown used to the fact that there were no half-mad Frenchmen. Did he have a passport or had he thrown everything away, lost it? Had he run out of the house in his underwear and then received clothes from good-hearted people on the way? But perhaps there was nothing wrong and he was just a lonely musician who had been turned out from where he sawed away at his fiddle or gave lessons to young ladies or composed just for himself, dreaming of world acclaim?

But these thoughts came and went, and life went on without interruption. This Sunday was nothing at all like the last, when they had sat in the garden over the samovar with the Kreins. No one came from town. Chabarov and Daunou arrived at five o'clock on bicycles. The three of them sat in Vassily Georgievich's study for a long time and talked, about the war, of course, but in a different way than they had the week before: they were talking about their hopes. Daunou talked about his own hopes, about how they could still put a stop to this insane, iron advance at the Seine and the Marne. Each time Maria Leonidovna looked in on them she had the feeling that the Frenchman wanted to tell her something. He got up and spoke to her in particular, and for some reason she found that unpleasant. He gave her the impression (only her, though) of being an hysteric, and when she left the room she was afraid of running into him later in the dining room, the yard, the garden.

She couldn't have explained her feeling, but Daunou's serious, determined, overly expressive face was before her all the time. She started to make tea, and he came out into the dining room, closing the door behind him as if in despair, and Maria Leonidovna felt that he was about to tell her something she would remember the rest of her life.

'*Nous sommes perdus, madame,*' he said quietly, looking into her face with his small eyes of indeterminate colour. 'Even the Emperor Napoleon himself, whom I wanted to resurrect last Sunday, couldn't do anything now. I'm telling only you this. You make your own decision about where and when you should leave. *Paris est sacrifié.*'

He turned white. His face contorted. But he coughed awkwardly, and everything fell into place again. She was left, frozen, holding the porcelain sugar bowl.

'There will not be a battle on the Loire. The Maginot Line will be taken from the west. Nothing at all is going to happen. It's all over. They'll go all the way to Bordeaux, to the Pyrénées. And then we'll sue for peace.'

At that moment Vassily Georgievich and Chabarov walked out into the dining room, and everyone sat down at the table.

She believed Daunou, but not completely, and for that reason when she and Vassily Georgievich were alone again she was unable to convince him that everything would be as Daunou had said. She said, 'You know, I think it would be best if you didn't go back to Paris again. Let's pack up tomorrow and move to the South, all three of us, Tuesday at the latest. We can spend a month or two in Provence, until things calm down. Like everyone else.'

He listened to her thoughtfully, but couldn't agree.

'What would they say about me at the office? They'd call me a coward. Tomorrow I'm going to Paris, and I give you my word of honour, I'll be back on Wednesday. Even if all's well, I'll be back. Haven't we seen plenty in our time? For them this is terrible, but we've seen a lot worse . . . "Nothing happens at a pace like that, a pace like that,"' he sang brightly.

The next day she was left alone again with Kiryusha. The traveller was still in the annexe.

He continued to get up late, sit by the window, and look out at the yard, at the trees, at the sky. Sitting erect, his hands placed on the windowsill, he looked and listened with a sad and equal attention both to the birds moving about in the lilac bushes and to the distant gunfire and the human talk beyond the gates and in the house. Once or twice he got up, put on his faded, outsize hat, or picked it up, and went out, softly shutting the gate. He walked through the village, taking a good look at what was going on, since every day the people got more and more worried, agitated, and grim. In the evenings he sat for a long time, no longer at the window but on the threshold to the annexe, his eyes half closed, his hand lazily resting on the head of the old dog, who came to sit next to him.

Night fell, the moon glimmered. There was something menacing about the clear sky, the quiet fields, the roads running to and fro, this summer, this world where fate had compelled him to live. When he rested his head on his hand, it seemed he was trying to remember something and that was why he was so quiet, that he couldn't do it. Where was he from? And where should he go, and did he have to go any farther? And what was life, this pulse, this breathing, this waiting, what was this ecstasy, this grief, this war? He was so weak, but he had a powerful harmony in his heart, a melody in his head. Why was he here among all this, among the now incessant noise of the gunfire, among these preparations for departure in village families, where they led out horses, tied up cows, where they sewed up gold into the lining of clothes? He had nothing. Not even a pack. No family, no lover to sew him a shirt, cook him soup, rumple and warm his bed. All he had was music. That's how he had grown up, that's how it had been since he was a child. Feet to carry him, hands to fend off people, and music, and that was it. But there was no point coming, no, no point coming into a world where he would always go unrecognised and unheard, where he was weaker than a shadow, poorer than a bird, as guileless as the simplest flower of the field.

When Kiryusha saw that the dog was sitting beside him and wasn't afraid, he came and sat as well, not daring to sit on the porch, but close by, on a stone. And so all three of them sat for a long time, in silence, until it got dark, and then Kiryusha, taking a deep breath, let out a long, idiotic laugh and went into the house.

IV

On Wednesday morning Vassily Georgievich did not come back. There had been no telephone communication with Paris for two days, and Maria Leonidovna had absolutely no idea what to think. People were saying that there weren't any trains, that the papers hadn't come out, that travel across Paris was impossible, and that people had been deserting Paris for two days. The entire village was packing up and leaving. Those who only the night before had criticised people fleeing from fear were themselves loading things onto carts, cars and perambulators. A swarm of little boys and girls sped around on bicycles. Three rows of small trucks and cars filed down the main road, which passed less than a mile from the village. During the day rumours had been flying around, the gunfire went on constantly, growing ever nearer, and silver aeroplanes sailed high in the sky. Several cars, trying to take a short cut, wound up on the avenue of plane trees and couldn't figure out how to get out, so they looped back and returned to the main road, nosing into the endless chain and continuing southward.

There were artillery, gypsy caravans, trucks loaded with ledgers (and on them sat pale bookkeepers, evacuating the bank, the foundation of the state); people on foot, on bicycles, broken-rank cavalrymen on light horses interspersed with percherons harnessed to long wagons carrying sewing machines, kitchen utensils, furniture, barrels. And high above all the goods and chattels were perched old women, deathly pale and bare-headed; some old women sat in cars, while others went on foot, alone or sup-ported by the arm. Troops hauled decrepit cannons and an empty van surmounted by a magnificent red cross followed behind a sports car out of which leaned a lop-eared dog that looked like a soft toy. Then came the wounded, some of them sitting despondently, holding on to their own leg or arm, a stump that dripped blood on the road. Others vomited air and saliva. People carried hay, unthreshed wheat, factory lathes, tanks of oil. And this odd stream could be seen all the way to the horizon, living and yet already dead.

Up until nightfall Maria Leonidovna cleaned and packed, fully aware that Vassily Georgievich couldn't come by train, just as they couldn't leave by train. From the house she could see the main road, and since morning she had watched the relentless, slowly flowing, sometimes pausing, river of fugitives. The thought that she might be left alone after everyone was gone worried her, and above all the thought that Vassily Georgievich might not return. She was worried as well about Kiryusha, who in the rising panic had suddenly become grotesquely incoherent. In the middle of the day she saw her silent guest a few times, and even greeted him from a distance. She resolved to have a chat with him, find out about him, maybe help him out, and that decision preoccupied her for a few minutes. The evening came, she prepared supper, and just as they were sitting down she heard the sound of a motor, a comforting, familiar sound. Two cars drove into the Sushkovs' yard: in one sat the three Kreins; in the other, Edouard Zontag, Vassily Georgievich, and old Mrs Sushkova. Both cars had left Paris the previous evening. They had been on the road all night and all day.

Manyura Krein broke down in tears when she walked into the house. 'This is too much! Simply too much!' she said with her large mouth. 'This is not to be endured. Children are being led along on foot, old people are hobbling on crutches. I'll never forget this as long as I live.'

But Maria Leonidovna scarcely got to hug her because she had to say hello to Zontag and to Magdalena and follow her husband into the next room and listen to his agitated story about how yesterday afternoon he had realised that she was right, that they should have left on Sunday, that now they might not make it.

'Kiryusha's not too good,' she told him, since even today she considered that that was the most important thing.

Edouard Zontag had longstanding business ties with Vassily Georgievich, and relations between them, for some reason only they understood, were rather strained. He kept aloof, apparently looking on the Kreins as relatives of Maria Leonidovna, and smoked a fat cigar. He was short and used to say that the shorter the man, the fatter the cigar he smoked.

An omelette, cold meat, salad, cheese, an apple tart, just appeared on the table, all at once, and they launched into it haphazardly and greedily, letting the abundance of that house fill them with contentment, fully aware that tomorrow it would all be gone. They drank a lot and talked a lot. They discussed how and when the decision had been made to surrender Paris, the bombing of its northern and western suburbs, and especially how everyone had dropped everything and fled, not only those who had been preparing for it but also those who had had no desire whatsoever to budge; how that night, in total darkness, it took them five hours to get from their apartment to the city limits. How they had been surrounded by thousands upon thousands of others like themselves, how the engine died on them, the radiator boiled over, and they took turns sleeping.

Then they had a conference: what time tomorrow should they go and which road was best? They bent over the map for a long time, sketched something, drew it out, and then drank again and even had another bite to eat, especially the men. In the yard an old lady slaughtered two hens, and Manyura cleaned them on the big kitchen table, lowered her fingers, covered in rings, with varnished nails, down into it, and drew out something slippery. Magdalena and Maria Leonidovna, sitting on their heels by the linen closet, looked for one more pillowcase for Edouard. The men were trying to decide whether or not to drive over to pick up Chabarov, and old Mrs Sushkova wanted to express her opinion too, but no one was listening to her.

She went to her room, that is, to Kiryusha's room, where she was supposed to spend the night, and it immediately began to reek of her perfume in there. Room was found for the Kreins in the house, but Edouard Zontag had to be put in the annexe.

'Wait for me, I'll be back in a minute,' said Maria Leonidovna, and she ran across the yard.

She knocked on the door. He was lying on the bed but not sleeping, and when she came in he raised himself and slowly lowered his long legs in their torn boots and ran his hand over his hair, as if he wanted to smooth it, comb it, give it some semblance of order. She started speaking softly, scarcely glancing in his direction.

'Excuse me, but something's come up. We have a full house. People didn't sleep last night, and there's nowhere to put them. Please, we have a small shed by the garage. Move over there. I feel bad disturbing you, but you understand, there's nothing else I can do. And then, in any case, we'll be leaving early tomorrow morning and you'll have to leave too because we'll be locking up and taking the keys with us. You won't be able to stay.'

He stood up and in the semi-dark (a cold bleak light fell from the entryway where a small lamp was lit) started pacing around the room, evidently at a loss how best to answer her.

'Tomorrow morning? Then why move to the shed? I'll leave tonight.'

She couldn't help feeling glad that he'd said this.

'I feel that I'm chasing you away, practically in the middle of the night. Please stay. There's a folding bed in there. And tomorrow morning — '

'No, I'll go right now. After all, everyone else seems to be leaving, don't they?'

'Yes, if they haven't already.'

'So I think I'd better go as well. Thank you for letting me spend so many days with you. Really, I'm most grateful to you. There are many people who wouldn't have done it, you know. I'll remember it for a long time, a very long time.'

He turned out to have a thick stick, which he must have cut in the forest the day before. His eyes met Maria Leonidovna's, and his look confused her.

'Wait a moment, I'll bring you something.' She turned around and lightly stepped out.

'That's not necessary. I don't need anything,' he shouted firmly. 'Don't worry, please. Goodbye.'

In the yard the men were tying something to the roof of the Kreins' car. She ran into the house, pulled fifty francs out of her purse, wrapped the remains of the roast beef and two rolls in a napkin, and went back to the annexe. The little lamp was still burning inside the door, but there was no one there now. He had left quietly, so that no one would notice, and very quickly. In the room it was as if he had never even stayed there; not a single object was out of place.

She looked around, as if he might still be standing somewhere in a corner. She walked out, went back in again, and then walked to the gate and opened it. Someone was walking alone down the lane – already quite a way away. She watched him for a moment, and suddenly, for no reason, tears came to her eyes, and she couldn't see anything.

'He's leaving, he's leaving,' she said very quietly but distinctly, the way people sometimes utter a meaningless word, and burst into tears. And without understanding what was wrong, or why she had suddenly been overcome by such weakness, she closed the gate gently and went into the house.

In the morning a life began that had nothing to do either with the departed guest or with Maria Leonidovna's secret thoughts. They loaded up the cars so that the spare tyre bumped along behind them on the ground. They locked up the house and sat Kiryusha between his father and grandmother – that day he had exhibited the early signs of rebellion, and they were trying to conceal it. Edouard Zontag, in good form after a night's sleep, was worried that they hadn't taken enough petrol. He took one more long look at the map before setting off. In the first car rode the Kreins and Maria

Leonidovna. Manyura rattled on incessantly.

They drove through the deserted village slowly, with difficulty, the spare tyre constantly bumping against the road. When they reached the forest, they started taking country lanes heading in the direction of Blois. They stopped by the château where Chabarov worked as a groundsman. The iron gates were wide open, and horses, still saddled, grazed on the English lawn between young cedars. A French squadron had been stationed there since the previous day. Soldiers were lying on the grass in front of the house and on the ground floor a vast hall, with two rows of windows, and its candelabra, mirrors and bronzes, could be glimpsed through the broken panes.

Chabarov came out wearing corduroy trousers and a matching jacket. The lower half of his face was covered with grey whiskers. Without even saying good morning, he said that he couldn't leave, that he had to stay behind: the night before Daunou (who lived in a nearby hamlet) had been found dead. He had shot himself, and since there was no one left in the area to bury him, Chabarov had decided to bury the body in his garden.

'If these brave lads,' he said gloomily, pointing to the soldiers, 'stay until evening and I manage to dig a suitable hole, then they'll be my witnesses, and that's the best I can hope for. But if they set off before then I'll have to wait for the new authorities to get here. There's no civilian population left.'

Everyone became very quiet as they said goodbye. Krein even got out of the car to embrace him. A minute later both cars drove off downhill, heavy with their loads, following each other closely.

That day, the sound of gunfire came from the other direction, from the northwest. In the sky, with a noise that had not been heard before, like a wail, swooped two German fighter planes.

The Waiter And The Slut

I

She was the daughter of a Petersburg bureaucrat who had risen to the rank of full councillor of state – a distrustful, unhealthy and discontented man with a long, thin face. Her mother was so like the wives of other Petersburg bureaucrats that after she died Tania, who was nearly fifteen, was unable to distinguish in her memory between her and all the other ladies who used to visit, pinch Tania's little chin, and chat – shrieking with laughter and toying with their lorgnettes – about their servants, the shops, their charity committees.

A governess was brought into the house, but she didn't get on, as she couldn't control Lila, the eldest, who used to be met after school by a naval cadet. Tania and Lila taught her to drink Madeira and curse in Russian, and they assured her that the downstairs lodger was madly in love with her. One day when everyone was out the governess surreptitiously packed her things, put them in a cab, and departed, having left His Excellency a note saying she just couldn't cope any longer.

That was a year before the Revolution. Her father was assigned to Siberia, so all three of them moved to Irkutsk. The fourth in their party was Ella Martynovna, their mother's old governess, a dry old stick whose once flirtatious eyes had now grown dim. The sideboards, the grand piano, the two Shishkin copies, and the French rugs travelled with them too. And in Irkutsk, in their enormous official apartment, among new faces and new amusements, their haphazard life started up all over again.

Ella Martynovna was cool towards Tania's father. However, he struck up an affair almost immediately with the vice-governor's wife – although it was more than an affair, and soon became a nerve-racking and interminable romance. The vice-governor's wife, who was old and fat, and the chevalier of the Order of Stanislas met in the secluded lanes of the municipal garden or on the edge of town, on the banks of the deserted Angara. Sometimes they chose a moonlit night and, if it wasn't too damp, sat on the grass or on a dead tree-stump. They played at youth, at Maupassant, at the forbidden, and the whole town laughed behind their backs at his frock coat and her pince-nez.

At the same time, in a smoky *shashlik* restaurant, a clarinet was wailing, and a bold, wasp-waisted Circassian woman was dancing the *lezginka*. And Lila, crossing her legs high (while an Armenian acquaintance held her closely), pulled on a cigarette, choked on the smoke, squinted, lifted her little finger from her wet glass, and then slipped into the toilets to make her eyes even blacker and give herself yet another spray of perfume.

On those nights Tania would sit at home and brood. She thought about what dream she might build for herself. What should she be? Her life was just about to start and she had to prepare for it, not miss her chance, not make mistakes. Get married as quickly as possible? Become a diva? Or a writer, setting down the story of her inner life? Ella Martynovna moistened her long gnarled finger and read Tania's cards, and it always came out the same: someone tried to ruin her, someone envied her, someone stood in her way, but she overcame all those obstacles to be joined in holy matrimony to a dark man with a large fortune.

Another departure. This time with no sideboards and no Shishkins. Departure for Japan. Escape. From whom? Among others, from the vice-governor's wife, but chiefly from the Bolsheviks. Tsarist banknotes were sewn into corsets – one for Tania, one for Lila, and one for Ella Martynovna. And in their corsets crackling with banknotes and wearing heavy frock coats weighed down on one side, it was the four of them again, as if they were the closest of families, unable to live apart. They were going to Nagasaki, they were running away. On the ship, to the courteous murmurings of the Japanese, Lila vomited blood and had to go below and lie down. Late at night Tania stood on the deck amid bags and boxes, pinned to the railing by an elderly engineer's kiss, and suddenly understood – without Lila she felt a hundred times happier, freer, and easier. Without Lila everyone liked her. It was just that there was no life for her when Lila was at her side.

Lila was beautiful, but when they arrived in Japan Tania noticed that her vitality began to seep away, and even her face – regular, pale, long – grew stern and bored. In the mornings Lila did a lot of praying, and the medallion she wore held a portrait of the Tsar. By spring she had given in altogether, and no longer dressed up, or allowed herself to be kissed. She tied her hair up at the nape in a severe bun and was fond of saying that even a life dedicated to prayer would not be enough to absolve Russia.

'I congratulate you!' her sister exclaimed.

Tania had small, well-spaced teeth and soft, extraordinarily soft skin – even as an adolescent she had had no blemishes on her body. She had freckles and a broad nose beneath her narrow, heavy-lidded eyes, and the oval shape of her broad face was off-centre. She was short, with a large bust. Her hands were big and strong, and her walk was lopsided. But within a few months Tania had men swarming around her, men who told each other candidly that she had a special way of giving her entire body when you kissed her. Now no one was paying any attention to Lila, and there was a persistent rumour going around that she was going to be thirty soon.

But among the men who brayed with laughter at weak jokes and ate too much, who sang Tania love songs, and seized her in their arms, there was one by the name of Alexei Ivanovich. Alexei Ivanovich had trained for counterintelligence and so knew Japanese, and he was now working in a

Japanese bank, a meek man and painfully fastidious about using other people's forks and glasses. He had large, fixed, almost blue eyes and a silly black moustache that looked as if it had been drawn on. He came and went with the others. But one day Ella Martynovna said, 'The king of clubs has confessed to the king of diamonds that Taniusha is divine but he's really in love with Lilisha.' In fact, for some reason Alexei Ivanovich had imagined that the girl with the tragic knot of hair and the unhealthy complexion whom he had twice glimpsed in the hallway was precisely the celestial vision that he had been waiting for all his life. The next day Lila, after having powdered her cartilaginous nose, pinned a porcelain bird to her breast, and came out to the guests. She nodded her head, twisted her long bony hands, coughed in a particularly significant way, and a month later Alexei Ivanovich proposed.

For the first time, Tania lost her head. She couldn't sleep at night. She threw her arms over her head, grabbed the headboard, and arched her whole body until she was numb. It was inconceivable to her, incredible, that anyone could prefer Lila to her. Whether or not she liked Alexei Ivanovich she didn't know, he was the only one among all the men who visited them who hadn't tried to kiss her and fondle her, who hadn't whispered obscenities to her, who, in short, had paid her absolutely no attention. The thought that someone had slipped through her fingers, that life was beginning with a defeat, was intolerable to her. The black moustache and the fixed eyes were transformed for her into an unexpected temptation.

She went to see him at about nine one Saturday morning. He had just dressed and was still walking around the room in his bare feet (this turned out later to be a habit).

'So good to see you, Tatiana Arkadievna. I'm flattered. To what do I owe this pleasure?'

Smiling, he drew up the armchair for her with his large white hands. In her fur coat and fur cap, she looked in astonishment at his clean bare feet.

'I came on a bet,' she said, still not knowing how she was going to get through this. 'I had a little bet with myself.'

He laughed out loud. 'With yourself . . . ' he echoed, utterly oblivious to how upset she was.

'Look,' she said in a low voice, and she flung her coat open.

Her stockings stopped at wide satin garters (bought the day before), and below them came the rumpled flounces of her beribboned drawers – and that was it. There was nothing else on Tania's body; her soft, extraordinarily soft skin had a blue shade to it, and the nipples and shadows under her breasts were orange-coloured. She sat without moving for several moments, her legs pressed firmly together and one stocking pulled up higher than the other. Then suddenly she made a single movement. She couldn't remember quite where she had got it from – whether it was Maupassant again or just Krinitsky, or even the nameless author of a book she'd devoured back in Petersburg. But the essential part came from herself: by her moans and spasms she showed Alexei Ivanovich the kind of passion she had learned in her dreams.

It always seemed to Alexei Ivanovich that life meant proceeding as cautiously as possible and, principally, watching his step – to keep from falling into some trap. Death was one of those traps, and everything that changed life unexpectedly, untowardly, was a trap – the Revolution he pictured as a hole into which his brother and father had fallen and which he himself had skirted. But there were further unknown traps where the foot could slip.

The next day his passion for Tania seemed to him to be one of these terrifying abysses, into which he had fallen with a dreadful crash, barefoot, his face contorted, his shirt ripped, hurtling down God knows how many steps on his knees and cracking his head on a stoop he couldn't see – this was his headboard, against which he banged his forehead until he nearly passed out from pain, fury and happiness. A week later he had regained his meekness, his smile, and the mica-like glint in his large eyes. He married Tania and took her to Shanghai. There was a lost look to his face and his trembling body seemed suddenly much thinner.

She was pleased with her husband and Shanghai and the fact that she had left home, and her nine years with Alexei Ivanovich – during which she had a brief affair with an American and an unhappy romance with a married Russian, produced a stillborn daughter, and visited her father once – passed peacefully, for she never thought about the present, and if she thought at all, it was about the future. The years passed utterly without trace. There was nothing in Japan which could remind her of her youth. Her father was paralysed, and Lila was working as a translator in an export office. She had grown old and ugly. Ella Martynovna was no longer among the living. At the end of the ninth year Tania decided she wanted to go to Paris, where many other people seemed to be going, and Alexei Ivanovich decided that he wanted to go to Paris too – in any case, he always wanted the same things as she did. He had thought it all out very carefully (which demanded a considerable effort), and left his job. So they left – to look for happiness, as Tania put it, calculating her chances, imagining the future. But it wasn't entirely clear just how she pictured that happiness, her own happiness in particular, her own and Alexei Ivanovich's Parisian happiness.

The trump card that Alexei Ivanovich hoped to play in Paris was his knowledge of Japanese, which he believed would stand them in good stead. But four months later, when their money ran out, he still didn't have a job, and they had nothing but complications with visas and passports and the French language, which neither of them knew, and Alexei Ivanovich began to have fits, during which he hurled and smashed everything within reach, cursed and swore, and became completely insomniac. Sleepless and barefoot he paced around the room of the small hotel in which they lived, and Tania beat her head against the pillows. Soon after, on a visit to some of his relatives (the host, a former hussar, was now a priest), he had his last fit.

It happened out in the suburbs. The house stood in the middle of a damp, narrow garden. The window was open, and flies flew at the lamp, burned themselves, and fell into the jam pot. It was all very much like Russia: a brass samovar stood on the edge of the table, and they poured boiling water into it from a kettle they heated on the stove. The priest's wife, with her pink nails and bleached blonde hair, was telling stories about some grand people that no one had ever heard of. The guests were drinking tea, and one tiny slice of apple pie was left on the plate.

Suddenly Alexei Ivanovich interrupted his hostess and in a sobbing, powerful voice announced that he was hot. 'Go and sit by the window,' said the hussar priest. 'The evening breeze will soothe your weary body.' But Alexei Ivanovich jumped up and shouted that he wouldn't be tricked into going near that window. 'Not on your life. You're not going to make me fall out!' Several of them gave him a troubled look, but in a flash he had torn off his jacket, waistcoat and trousers and had already pulled off one shoe before they seized him. His clear blue eyes were glittering, and he was now dressed only in white, but he grew meek again and smiled, smoothing his silly black moustache. However, he then began to beat them off so savagely that they had had to call an ambulance. Two orderlies came and leapt on him, knocked him off his feet, piled on top of him, and dragged him down the road while, delirious, he shouted incomprehensibly.

A few days later he died in the hospital — swollen from beatings, his hair almost grey, his front teeth knocked out — in a ward for the dangerously insane. And Tania found herself alone in a cheap hotel room in Paris, where she had come to 'look for happiness'.

She was on her own now. Each new day began, grey like her life. She didn't want that kind of day or that kind of night, long, lifeless, passed in making calculations in her head: how much money was left, what could she buy for that much, and where could she find the kind of man she could hide behind, who would take care of everything, and pay for everything, and give her presents, and worship her, as it happened probably for everybody, as it had for two of her girlfriends from Petersburg that she'd run into here and for one from Shanghai, in short, for the women she thought she knew. The day began, and she started to visit shops, rarely buying anything but choosing, checking prices, digging through the stockings and gloves, begrudging the money, and in her dreams becoming so excited that her heart pounded as she pictured herself in this silk or that fur. She sifted through piles of lace and let buttons stream through her fingers, always hesitant and fearful of buying the wrong things, continuing to wear her worn red fox with the thick tail trailing off her shoulder and her dusty black hat with the black flower, which was supposed to signify mourning. She was thirty-two. Since her marriage and the dead baby she had put on weight, but her face was still just as fresh as ever. Even now, carelessly and vulgarly made up, it attracted notice.

Once in a while she visited her Nadias, Marusias and Tatochkas, and one or another would give her something: a pair of laddered stockings, an old purse with a broken mirror. In the middle of a rapid and chaotic stream of chatter, one or another would reveal a corner of her life, and the wild abandon of passion, money, idleness, pampering and happiness took Tania's breath away; she clutched at those crumbs, seized them and carried them back with her to her room where she spent the night trying to work out what life really was – not her life but theirs, where everything was so gay, solid and calm. Then she went to see others who gave her nothing, who lived poorly and worked. Among them was Belova, a seamstress, and the topic of conversation at her place was always the same: what are the fashions? And how do you dress as cheaply and as well as possible? Tania's heart skipped a beat at hearing that one tiny mistake – a sleeve set in the wrong way or a badly cut collar – could ruin the appearance of a dress – and your whole fate with it. There was another, a tall, peroxided, bitter woman named Gulia who had tried her hand at dozens of professions. At one time she had gone to beauty school and been a model, but then syphilis and two miscarriages took the fight out of her and left her numb. Now she was a waitress in a restaurant where she broke the plates and cursed the customers.

Meanwhile Tania kept going to their houses, to the shops, through the streets, staring at the women she passed to the point of stupefaction, listening to their talk, which

she didn't always understand, mentally
trying on and fitting until she was utterly
exhausted, spending sleepless nights sorting
through all she'd seen and heard that day.
Nadia told her: 'My dear, first of all you have
to learn to wash. You simply don't know
how to wash.' Belova swore that she had to
dye her hair red and wear nothing but black.
Another pleaded with her to lose weight. But
all this revealed was their indifference, their
contempt for her. Only Gulia never gave her
advice, although doubtless she knew better
than any of them what Tania should do.

So, a little at a time, without confiding in
anyone, Tania began to transform herself,
always keeping in mind that she had only
enough money and skill to make herself one
single outfit to go . . . where? To the Russian
restaurant where they sang the 'Charochka',
and to another where they ate sturgeon and
grouse, and, last, to a third, a bar where the
music was Argentinian, not Russian, and
where Tania – alone, at night, with her gentle
face, large breasts, and her soft mouth –
fiddled with her long nails, sipped something
cold and alcoholic through a straw, and tried
not to look around her.

But she was not allowed to enter the
fashionable and well-reputed restaurant,

either because she was alone or because you had to tip the maître d' for the privilege of an introduction. An arm stopped her at the door, and a velvety baritone asked her – in French, but with a Russian accent – to leave. She was so distraught that she lost her voice. Unable to control herself, she started to weep and walked out. While she was deciding how to get home, a high-spirited character in a cape and top hat called her '*charmante*' and kissed the air a couple of inches from her cheek.

A passing car splashed her with dirty water. It was too late to go anywhere else, as it was midnight, so she went home and, sitting on her bed, sobbed with rage. The mascara in her tears stained her dress, and she started to clean it with lighter fluid but ruined the whole thing in the process, and felt like throwing herself out of the window. But her room was on the third floor (she always remembered that subsequently and never considered that solution again), and opened out over a courtyard which smelled so bad that she shut the window again immediately.

The next day she went to a restaurant which had no music and no gypsies, but was simply very expensive. As she crossed the room she caught a glimpse of a menu on one table and saw that there was a hundred-franc minimum. Men who reminded her of her father – bald, bearded, chewing voraciously or already digesting – sat with their backs to the walls paying her no heed whatsoever. In despair she looked at a pop-eyed, middle-aged gentleman picking his teeth, realised that no one here had the slightest use for her, and said she just needed to use the phone.

She went out and knew there was only one place left for her to go: that noisy, rowdy gypsy bar which Tata had told her about. She went there. She was hungry. A band greeted her. She was seated in a corner, and solicitously relieved of her ermine-trimmed coat, her entire fortune. She could tell immediately that this was where she was going to find what she had been looking for, if only for the time being. It might not happen today, or even tomorrow, but it was going to happen, and it was going to happen here.

A violinist dressed as a Romanian and a singer dressed as a gypsy wailed over her head. A steamy smoky haze hung from the ceiling. Couples floated past her table. Setting down her white hand which held a long cigarette holder, and thrusting out her generous, tightly swathed breasts, her petalled face glowing in the restaurant's darkness, she sat and looked without seeing. And in her waiting, in her secret hunger which, over the last few weeks, had almost given her a pain deep down in her body, there was something which evoked the languor of a sweet young girl on a moonlit, jasmine-scented evening standing at the window of her parents' sleeping house. Her indefinable thirst was overwhelming and, in the same way, the future ahead of her seemed misty, rose-coloured and terrifying.

Later, when she had put her coarse, degrading affair with the Romanian fiddler behind her, she remembered him not as a man, but as an animal. After a year and a half of shared life, eaten up by melancholy, jealousy, and fear of the next day, she left hospital — where she had had an operation — thin, poor, with huge eyes burning with bitterness and lucidity (the fiddler was no longer there, he had joined up with a band and left for London), and she went back to the same bar, finally understanding that no one loved or adored anyone until death separated them; that there was no one to hide behind; and that what had happened to her had happened to all her Tatas and Nadias, but none of them ever let on; she understood that you had to lie and lie and lie some more, take everything you could from life and do your best to forget, drink, erase your mistake and the concession you had made to that black-eyed rat who had sold you a few times and then left you.

It was only once in a while now, in the morning, roused at dawn by the early noise in the stinking narrow courtyard, that she ran back over those months, bitterly, unrestrainedly, back to what at first had been a gypsy love song, like fire flowing through her veins, sung in a low voice straight to her heart, and which later had given off the smell of unchanged sheets, the stink of city sewers on a raw November day when some yellow and foul-smelling liquid runs down into the gutters, something you fear to step in and let your heel sink into. She would lie in this way for an hour or two immersed in these memories, avoiding any others, and then fall into a deep sleep. During the day she tried to retrieve that lost feeling, that long-gone frame of mind that had once led her – after Alexei Ivanovich's death – in search of something she couldn't give a name to but without which she couldn't imagine living in the world. This indispensable thing consisted of idleness and physical pleasure, in other words, in her private language, Parisian happiness.

But in the evenings she went back to the only place left in the world, there was nowhere else for her, that gypsy bar. And there were moments as she sat there in the smoky air, listening to the uproar of the music, when she forgot to shed her habitual expression of hurt, sadness and suffering. The hand held out to her across the table – a short, sturdy, man's hand holding an open cigarette case – belonged to a man who liked in her precisely that weary and distraught face. She accepted a cigarette, took the cigarette case from him, and put it down on the tablecloth. Suddenly she squeezed that hand and, through her tears, smiled inquisitively.

'What could be better than a Russian woman!' exclaimed the man with an accent. 'No, tell me, please, what could be more charming, more luxuriant, more magnificent than a Russian woman?' And with a drum roll and a wail the music seemed to echo that question just to please the customer.

Four years. Three times a week – in the afternoon – he came to 'take a break' from the Stock Exchange, his wife, bridge, the unpaid bills, bounced cheques, and crises – his whole hard, busy, masculine life. Each time he left her a hundred francs and said that only here, in this cheap, grimy, welcoming room, did he feel like a human being and not a brute. 'Will he marry me?' she wondered sometimes. 'Get a divorce? Leave his wife?' Sometimes she asked him to take her out. But what if someone saw them together and exposed them? That would wreck his life. No, he was careful, and as soon as he arrived demanded his dressing gown and slippers, told her to put the tea on, and unwrapped the pastries. 'He's not going to marry me. He's never going to marry me,' she told herself at night, staring with hatred at his red dressing gown with the tassels that hung behind the door, that gave off his smell in the room, that guarded his goods. How happy she had been that day when he had brought that smell of his to her, brought his pyjamas and slippers. It was as if he had practically moved in; a little bit more and she would have had him completely in her power.

'Get a gun,' Gulia said one day. 'Just shake him up a little. Just imagine, what if a car ran over him? You'd be back where you started, like before. And you're getting older . . . '

She didn't threaten him with a gun, and towards the end of the fourth year he disappeared. He had said he would be out of Paris for a week on business, but almost a month passed and he still hadn't come back. The home address she had for him turned out to be wrong. There wasn't any house with that number on that street. She had the phone number of his club, so she called, but they told her he hadn't been in for over six months.

She lost her head, scoured the town, felt like running to the police. She had practically no money left, she had borrowed in order to pay for her room, and she was alone again. 'That pig didn't even give me enough to put some aside,' she thought. In anger and desperation, unwashed, her hair uncombed, she went to see Gulia. 'You're at home? You're not at work?' Gulia was sitting by the window holding a kitten on her fat knees and cross-stitching. They had let her go at the restaurant; now she was taking in embroidery.

'You could too if you wanted,' she said in her husky voice, while ashes from her cigarette dropped on the red embroidery wool and sky-blue canvas. 'You could make ninety centimes an hour. At least you wouldn't starve to death.'

'What about those other women?' Tania thought. 'The slim, chic, contented, happy women who work somewhere as secretaries and salesgirls, sleep with their bosses, go skiing, and buy all those smart clothes? Why not me?' In the dark shop windows she took a look at herself, tear-stained, older now, with sagging breasts and hips, walking her lopsided walk, gloveless. 'They just don't exist, that's all,' she told herself. 'For a month or two maybe. Liars. They're all useless. Like me.' Tears streamed down her face, and she wiped them away.

Restaurants? She knew them all now. That gypsy bar had closed, and another had opened in its place. The smart restaurant they hadn't let her into that time was the same as ever – Tatochka's lover had taken her there once. She had eaten with Nadia a few times at the restaurant where the men had intimidated her so much before: but the men, even if they weren't young and reminded her of her father, were finally just like any other men when you came right down to it, and a few of them had even stared at Nadia and her.

But she couldn't go there wearing an old girdle and with only a hundred francs in her purse. For a few more days she ran around town, stopped in to see Gulia a few more times, and started embroidering.

The first day she made nine francs; the second, eleven. She stayed in bed and cried nearly all of the third day, made four francs, and collapsed back into bed, her eyes all puffy. On the fourth day she bought half a lobster for seven fifty and ate it with mayonnaise. By the evening of the fourth day she was as good as drunk. It didn't even register with her when the landlady told her she shouldn't worry about paying for the room, she could take her time. On the fifth day she went to see Gulia on foot; she didn't have enough for the Metro, and she hadn't eaten. Gulia didn't have any work, but she did give her some coffee.

That same evening Tania borrowed a hundred and fifty francs from Nadia, a hundred-franc note and fifty in change, had dinner with her, listened to her stream of boastful lies, responded with the same, and in the morning, having spent three francs on food, started thinking what she should do. Her hands shook as she counted out the money. She had two plans, and one precluded the other.

The first was to buy a gun with the money, gorge herself, and then commit suicide. The second was to go to the hairdresser, get her hair done, have a pedicure, put on a becoming dress, and go somewhere to eat – but so that someone else was sure to pay for her and they would leave the restaurant together. She went over to the mirror and made the face she usually made when she looked at herself and that she never made at any other time. So, with all the will she could muster, she took herself in hand.

It was eight fifteen. She was a little late. She never managed to get anywhere on time. She was wearing a black dress, and a black hat that showed her curled, upswept hair above its top; she had dyed it red recently, but the black roots were already starting to show at the temples. The collar of her seal-fur coat covered her fat white neck, and when she turned it back a warm perfumed column of air escaped and fogged up around her face. Her last intact pair of stockings formed a web over her feet; she wore her light, open shoes. She went to the mirror again and made that face – content, calm, the face she would have liked to have. She looked at herself for a long time. Beautiful. She could have done with a little dog, one more pretext for making friends. 'Fool! Why didn't you get your Jew to give you a dog right at the beginning, when he was so kind?' Kind? Yes, he had been kind during the first and second years of their . . . love, shall we say, when he had given her the fur coat and put up with all her whims, her suspicions, her ugly face in tears. Later, when she started to reproach him for not marrying her and threatening to cling to him, he stopped being kind. And he was right. 'I could have held back. It's my fault,' she told herself quickly. 'Oh, you stupid, hopeless fool!' She was alone with her reflection. She reached for the door to the creaky aspen cupboard, swung it open, and shut it. 'He was kind, he was good, and he could have kept on being that way.' She seemed to be reading from inside herself, but there was something else. 'And now you're either going to take in embroidery or walk the streets.' She covered the mirror with her hand to hide the expression of her mouth. 'You're in deep water and you don't know how to swim,' she read on, aloud. Just then she saw her contorted face again. Her confidence in herself, in the fact that what she was about to do was right, dissolved. Go to bed. Let yourself go. Buy half a bottle of brandy. Get drunk ... She dismissed those pitiful temptations, opened and closed her coat once more, and went out.

When Tania entered the restaurant, which was decorated with a pretentious severity, it was two-thirds empty: in the corner to the right an elderly couple; on the left a younger couple; and beyond them more faces, men's, not so young, she thought (all this she had to take in in a few seconds). Three men busy with their hors d'oeuvres and vodka were sitting at the back. The maître d' wanted to seat her near the young couple by the door, but she walked right past him and sat down at the table next to the three men. Two waiters ran up to her, but she kept her coat on. Immediately a menu flew into her hands, a place setting materialised out of thin air, and she was left with no choice but to unfold her napkin.

'He was kind. He could have been kind,' she repeated to herself. She was drained after that long week. She remembered about her face, and smiled slightly to one side, but no one was looking at her. Meanwhile two more men (French, it seemed) came in and sat down across from her. But she felt she just couldn't cheer up, that she wanted to eat as quickly as possible and leave, that she needed to be left alone with her thoughts. 'Think things through. Get a good night's rest. But what about tomorrow?' flashed through her mind. 'Tomorrow I'll be like Gulia, or something else . . . I'll go to work. As a maid. Be a servant. These waiters running around here, they're servants.' She began watching one of them, a tall, middle-aged, balding man in a short white jacket. His hairy hands were busy with something over her place setting. 'He's brought the *selyanka*. He's serving the sturgeon.'

'Mushrooms for the table on the left,' a younger, pasty-faced waiter whispered to him as he hurried past, balancing clean glasses upside down between his fingers.

'Got it,' the bald man whispered back voicelessly. He served Tania her soup and ran off somewhere, swaying. She nearly lost him among four others who looked exactly like him. Her gaze followed him and she felt troubled. He reappeared, sailing through the air carrying a narrow platter of marinated mushrooms. He uncorked a napkin-wrapped bottle of wine and rolled the cheese trolley to the far corner. 'What does a man like that live for?' she asked herself. But the waiter kept flitting to and fro, carrying away dirty dishes. All of a sudden Tania saw him in the waiters' room close to her, greedily shovelling food from someone's plate into his mouth. She was disgusted.

'What does a man like that live for? My God, what for? But what am I living for? What does all of this mean?' she thought with pity for him and herself as well. 'What do people live for at all?' She tried to think for a moment. 'For pleasure. Yes, that's it. People live for pleasure. But what kind of pleasure is there in his life, or mine?'

'Didn't you like your sturgeon, madam?' he asked respectfully, seeing that she hadn't finished her *selyanka*.

'N-no, I did.'

With a deft motion of his hairy hands he whisked away the soup and something else and brought her a turkey wing on a silver oval platter. Standing very erect, he served it, moving only his wrists.

'Would you like a bottle of red wine?'

She ordered half a bottle of Nuits. One of the men sitting at the next table raised his wide-open, light brown eyes to her. For a moment he tried to recall something, to speak. 'Garçon! A bottle of Nuits here too,' he called out, finally realising what it was he needed. Tania turned away.

'What does a man like that live for?' she repeated to herself. 'Oh, my God, where is he? Here he is running and tottering with that gravy boat. What a tired old face he has. What a strange head. He must smoke a lot. He's smoked his teeth and heart out. But what am I living for? Why am I trying? Where does all this lead? Why will I die tomorrow and how? I've got to get a hold of myself. I'm not going to scheme or be jealous of anyone any more. I've got to stop.'

With inexplicable symmetry first the elderly and then the younger couple stood up. The little pot-bellied doorman with the skinny bowed legs helped them on with their coats. They left. Her neighbours asked for the bill, snatched the slip of paper away from one another, and overturned the carafe; finally the leader with the light brown eyes paid. Tania held a piece of frozen peach in her mouth for a long time and watched – not their faces but what they left for a tip and how the bald waiter, his face indifferent now, bent at the waist, picked up the money, and thanked them, quickly pulling their chairs out for them.

Then he passed them on to the maître d', the maître d' to the doorman, and the doorman – by this time on the street – to the taxi driver. Meanwhile the waiter's face had become its old self again.

'Coffee, please,' Tania said with only her lips.

There, that dinner was over, and she was going to pay for it herself. It was all very good. The place had certainly emptied out. There was the one with the pasty face and the other one, a little younger, hurrying by with a heap of napkins and once more with glasses, dirty ones this time, stems down. The Frenchmen were still there, it seemed, but now some ladies had joined them. She had missed them coming in: elegant, gay, lively. There they were, to have a good time. Here was the tall waiter again. He lit the flame under her café filtre.

'Not many people here,' said Tania. Even she didn't know why she said it. 'It's nice when there aren't so many people.'

'Quite. It's very nice.'

He walked away. The spirit lamp was burning, heating the coffee. He came back just in time.

'Are there more people at lunch?' (Why am I asking this? I won't be coming back here anyway.)

'I should say so. Sometimes they're still here at three.'

'It must be exhausting, isn't it?'

'You get used to it. I've been working here for over ten years.'

'What did you do before?'

He had already gone to fetch the sugar tongs, though, limping just a little. She watched his hairy fingers again, and she imagined she could see his thin, sunken, very hairy grey chest through his short jacket.

'Before? When exactly?' Dancing in circles around her, he attempted a confused smile.

'Before. In Russia.'

'I fought for my faith, my Tsar, and my motherland,' he said in a conspiratorial way.

She stirred her coffee and looked at him. He was standing to one side, at attention, as far as his round shoulders would permit.

'You're not from Petersburg, by any chance?'

'Indeed. Nikolaevsky Cavalry Academy.'

Something like a long corridor was taking shape in her mind, but she couldn't see what was at the end of it.

'I knew Akhlestov and Zaune from Nikolaevsky Academy. They used to come around to see my older sister.'

'I knew Akhlestov. He was four years below me.'

So. Now she would give him a chance to move away, to gather up the dessert dishes, one by one, and take them out to the waiters' station until tomorrow, come back, stand by the cashier, his napkin pressed under his arm, running his eyes over the last customers. Others were still scurrying around near the door. If she had sat by the window it wouldn't have been him waiting on her but, say, that putrid blond with the translucent nostrils. He could move away now: everything was clear, a slim, fragile link had already formed between them, through Lila and the outsized, long dead Akhlestov, of whom Tania had been so afraid when she was a little girl and who had once seized her to do a little dance with her, crudely rumpling her dress.

He looked in her direction. No, she still hadn't asked for the bill. He walked past her.

'Tell me,' she thought he wouldn't hear her murmur, but he did, and again he danced in circles around her, tilting his long head to one side. 'Maybe you knew my sister, Lila Shabunina? I'm Tania Shabunina. That's my maiden name. I've been married. No? And the Vertyaevs? (What a funny name!) We were there a lot. There were the Filantievs, too. They used to have Christmas parties, I remember, with lots of children. All of them were older than me; there's six years between my sister and me. The Filantievs. They lived near Chernyshev Bridge. There were also the von Gogens . . . My father served with Kirkilevich. You didn't know Kirkilevich? His daughter's married to Tsvetkov now. But from Nikolaevsky Academy, no. I do remember Okhotnikov from Konstantinovsky Artillery Academy. His father was a big shot.'

He slipped an ashtray under her burning cigarette.

'Is that so,' he replied mechanically. He bowed and scraped awkwardly and went to write out the bill. One of the round white chandeliers had been turned off, but Tania hadn't noticed.

'Listen,' the cashier said to him, 'your friend is holding us up. It's after ten.'

He flicked the bill and ran quickly to the waiters' station. He had a consuming, piercing need to be alone for a minute – solitude and quiet, and a chance to recall something, to reconstruct something . . .

He opened the door to the small cloakroom, which was dark and smelled of cabbage and old clothes. Here on small hangers were the waiters' dark jackets. He recognised his own by the special light grain of the wool. He clutched at his empty sleeve, crushed it, and thought.

He wanted passionately to reconstruct, but he didn't know how to do it. He was one of those people who, when they hear the phrase 'The windows of the house looked out on a garden', imagine an old house in the country that they once glimpsed somewhere and which has stood guard in their memory ever since. Whenever he heard the phrase 'The train pulled slowly into the station', he saw the same black locomotive which had already come to a halt by a water tank half in ruins, a sign in Polish on the glass of a station door, and the whitish blue of the horizon, which had palled over the long years. Anything that didn't have its own fixed image in his memory simply wouldn't stick and had slipped away long ago. But just now something odd had happened to him. The words 'Chernyshev Bridge' and 'Christmas party' had swept across his brain like an avalanche, and what remained in the column of dust and the roar of Tania's words had frozen in place, touching his heart. A slender little girl wearing a red dress has snatched a shimmering spun-glass ornament from a branch of the Christmas tree and is crushing it to powder in her thin sweaty fingers. He is in his uniform; he has washed carefully, and on his golden curls he's wearing a three-cornered cotton cap tilted over one ear – also freshly laundered. The glass dust spills over the girl's hands and dress. Maybe this lady sitting here and smoking, powdering her nose, maybe she's the same girl? No, of course she isn't. Then maybe she's her sister? No, things don't happen like that. Then it's someone she must have known, or seen. The Filantievs. That

was it. He couldn't remember anything else –
or make any other associations. But that was
enough: suddenly the sunny fragments of a
child's summer day, when he snagged his
jacket on the latch jumping out of the
window, rushed, rolled, washed over him.
Other days too – funny and sad, and
multicoloured, and so fast you couldn't hold
them back. Tight white gloves on his little
hands, and his long cadet's overcoat, and
something proud and awesome which happened after he had joined the Corps. The
wild and wonderful freedom of spring, and
again the azure December weather, and that
intersection near Exchange Bridge where for
some reason he always imagined an ocean
liner entering the Neva through the mists,
bursting its banks, and growing and growing
until it towered over the Peter and Paul
Fortress; and something else: sobbing
strident brass, the curl of regimental
trumpets over his father's coffin. Sand and
snow. And quiet. And in the black northern
sky a comet he had glimpsed one night from a
window. And something else, something . . .
before everything exploded into life, war,
promotions, boozing, marriage, escape.
Before it all led him to this office, to the
smoky gloom of the waiters' station, to

customers' plates with mustard smeared around the rim, to lettuce that stuck to his fingers, to the half-empty glasses which he'd drained. He squeezed and crushed the sleeve of his coat on its wooden hanger. He tugged at it, expecting a bell to ring, a tocsin to sound all over the universe, and maybe people would come running to him . . . But everything was quiet. The noises of footsteps and voices were muffled; all was quiet.

Then he opened the door and went back in.

She was sitting there as before, but now she was all alone in the half-darkened restaurant. Tablecloths were already being pulled off tables; the waiters were moving, gathering up chairs, crowding her out. The maître d', with his jacket off, was standing in front of the cash register, and the owner had turned up – a well-dressed Pole who pronounced his *r*'s like a Frenchman. There was a coloured handkerchief in his breast pocket, and he was whistling as he went over the accounts. She was still sitting there. She could have left, but she couldn't. Or rather, he couldn't let her; she had something to say to him, she was going to remind him of something. What a marvellous, soft, fleeting beauty there was in her face, and how strange – her eyes, her fingers, her voice. She had said 'Akhlestov'.

Who was Akhlestov? Maybe he was the one in '18 who . . . And now he had risen from the dead, risen and brought them together today, here.

He put Tania's bill in front of her.

'Allow me to introduce myself,' he said. 'Lieutenant Bologovsky.'

She put a hundred-franc note down on the table, slapped it with her hand, and raised her face.

'Delighted to meet you.'

He ran over to the cash register, got her change, and returned.

'Imagine meeting like this. Amazing. Did you leave long ago?' (Somehow he just had to. Still, could he possibly care whether it was ten, or fifteen, or however many years she'd been wandering around?)

'Oh, a long time ago!'

She took her change and left a tip. Wearing a frozen smile, he cocked his head in a signal to someone, and the pasty-faced waiter ran by and swept up the money with his big dark wrists, mumbling his thanks.

'Allow me.' And now he bowed, his head receded into his shoulders, and his back became narrow and rounded. 'Can we leave together? Lieutenant Bologovsky. Please do not take this for impertinence.'

'You mean you can go?'

'One moment.'

Now she saw that she should have left long ago. She opened and closed her compact again and took out her mirror. She was flushed from the wine and food.

He told her the story of his life, shortening the account of his marriage a little, but talking boastfully of his married daughter who lived in Bulgaria and who was always making plans to visit him but somehow never did. He told the story of his life in an hour, on the Metro and while they were drinking aniseed liqueur in a Russian bar somewhere in the fifteenth arrondissement, which was where he felt most at home. His heart was thundering, and his hands (in his haste he had forgotten to wash them) were shaking over the cigarette box, trying to introduce relative order to the table: here's her glass, here's mine; here are the cigarettes, there are the matches; here's her glove, black, warm, fragrant, and there's her hand – white, warm, fragrant. A woman was sitting before him. He couldn't quite remember how it had come about. He had had all sorts of different things to drink. His legs were sprawled out under the table, like boots, or like leggings, and he had a terrible urge to cry. It must be old age. He would not tell her how old he was – let her think forty-five; she could even think fifty, let her think what she wants.

He was looking at her breasts, at her hands, almost not looking at her face. And he was having a good time. But how could you remember all that had happened to you in your lifetime? What was I talking about? Oh, yes, my shaky, idiotic, painful past.

'I must confess, though, I have never spent an evening like this before. No, there's never been anything like it. Don't think I'm just trying to flatter you.'

'Even if you were,' said Tania, 'women love flattery. You're a man, you should know that.'

She was drinking too. By midnight he was talking about how hungry he was, so she ordered vodka and food as well, although only so that she would have something to eat with her three drinks. Two dark wide circles were forming around her eyes, and the vodka had made her mouth moist and deep. 'What is it he's playing at?' she asked herself in a drunken reverie. 'Matrimony, a one-night stand, or pimping for me? What if I asked him directly?'

The thought of that brought on a sudden fit

of shrill, tearful laughter. Her head bowed, she propped her face with both hands to keep it from falling on the table.

Her sudden inability to control herself aroused his passion and tenderness. She was sobbing hard. She picked up her glass and crushed it in her slender white fingers.

'For God's sake, Tatiana Arkadievna!' he exclaimed, breaking out in a sweat. 'You could cut yourself doing that.'

Her hands and dress were covered with shards of glass, but he could no longer speak. Clenching his fists under the table, a roar in his head and fire in his heart, he was sitting, and watching, and drowning in a happiness of which she was the cause. He couldn't remember a thing. He was trying not to breathe, not to blink, and in the haze of his bliss everything was intoxicating, pure, happy, and sad all at once.

She was bored though. The café, with the former governor of Kalouga behind the bar, was impregnated with grease and tobacco. The wire-stemmed paper tulip – which Bol-ogovsky kept fiddling with, not knowing where to put it, what to pair it off with – kept getting in her face. A photograph of a matador holding a guitar looked down at them from the wall. All this, and the man sitting with her, who had a tiny red insect crawling across his starched chest, seemed like such a comedown, such a terrible retribution, such a speedy path towards the end, that she wondered with anguish and horror how life could have dealt with her so brusquely and cruelly.

'If he tries to kiss me, I'll hit him hard in the face,' she resolved to herself.

But he squeezed both her hands in one big rough hand, and in the taxi he embraced her and touched her, pressing his harsh lips to hers, his hard face to hers. And a minute later she was filled with pity and tenderness for herself. What was she struggling for? Why? My God, it was all so sad. She tried to look at his eyes in the gloom, more out of habit than curiosity. Totally unfamiliar eyes glittered with metallic tears, and his sparse hair (he had removed his hat) seemed equally steely.

Silently he followed her upstairs, and there in her room, where it was such a mess, where a naked bulb hung from the ceiling and a chintz blind covered the window, he pushed her rudely and greedily, hurrying and falling (she was dawdling, as if she were thinking about something). But it didn't happen as he'd planned. Exhausted, drunk with her warmth, he fell into a heavy sleep, his face in the pillow.

II

Dishevelled, wearing a creased blue night-gown, black make-up smeared around her eyes, she lay in bed, dangling her arm almost to the floor. The silver bangle she wore was old, Russian. He was standing by the window in his coat. Outside was a courtyard three metres wide, an urban crevice, dank and dark. It was about to rain. Above him he saw other windows, but no matter how far you leaned over – no sky. Smoke was coming from somewhere above them and falling into this crevice. In his husky, sing-song voice, he recited:

> 'Rain, rain, run along,
> We are going to Arestan.'

She misunderstood the last word and echoed, yawning: 'We are going to a restaurant.'

He snorted, amused. Then he looked around, saw her, and, taking a few steps, planted a kiss on her head. Her red hair was fading and growing out; the parting was dark and streaked with grey.

'Please don't snivel,' she said, lifting her hand from the floor as if it were a dumb-bell. 'Well, what are you snivelling at now?'

He wasn't crying. He was looking down at her face, waiting for her to look up at him so that he could smile.

'You look like you're about to cry. Your eyelids are all red, there must be something the matter with your eyes. There's a tear running down your nose. But smile, God damn it. Aren't you having a good time?'

Cautiously he stroked her head and kissed her parting once more.

'My teeth are too bad for me to smile,' he said, and forced a laugh.

And in truth, why did he find it so intolerably sad to look at her? What did he regret? After all, the thing he hadn't dared hope for the first night they met had actually come to pass: she was with him; her body, her warmth were with him. He had a woman of his very own, and not one that just any man could have. She reminded him of something he'd once perceived as real but now saw more like a dream: sometimes (my God, if she ever found out) her smell, or the quick touch of her hand to his nape, reminded him of his mother. He left for work at eleven and returned at four, then went out again at six and came back at midnight. And she was always there. She saw him go; she waited for him to come back. She lay beside him in bed and warmed him, and he couldn't sleep for knowing that she was with him, that she had somehow managed to come back to him, bringing with her all he had lost.

'You know, Tania, my love, my sweetheart,' he said all of a sudden, 'I'm so happy I don't know what to make of it. And sad too. For some reason I keep thinking, why me? And you know, before I used to think, what am I? Why am I here? But now I've given all that up. I don't think about it any more.'

'The great philosopher.'

'Some philosopher with a face like mine. But none of that matters any more.'

'Thank heaven!' She vaguely recalled the day in the restaurant when, all alone, she had philosophised too.

'I'll be going now.' That was what he always said. It was as if he were working himself up to leave her. 'I have to. It's time.'

She stood up, threw on a short housecoat, belted it at the waist, and stood to wait for him by the door in her bare feet.

Then she lay down across the unmade bed and picked up yesterday's paper.

Before, she never so much as glanced at the paper. There were times when *he* had left her his — but she threw it out untouched. She didn't care about people she didn't know and never would. But for the past month, ever since Bologovsky moved in with her (and more and more often the conversation turned to what papers had to be filed before they could get married), ever since he had been with her, she had developed a taste for juicy crime stories reported in exquisite detail and with unusual verve, stories which always seemed to feature a blood-soaked sheet or a stiff towel stained by something suspicious, invariably foul-smelling — a lurid image that entranced Tania's imagination.

There were dramas that reminded her of a carcase being cut up in a butcher shop. And others — when a swollen body is pushed noiselessly into the water at night. Boxes are sent off to an unwitting recipient. People arm themselves with guns, kitchen knives, chisels. But the most burning and obsessive of all were the crimes inspired by a lie: the passage from arithmetic to algebra. Not just to destroy or be destroyed, but also to fool the whole world, even if you have to pay for it with your own life. Here's a woman who is jealous of her own daughter, and of her daughter's lover, whose wife she poisons. She is sentenced to life, but suspicion of a conspiracy falls on him too, something else (there's always a tiny something lurking in the background) comes into the picture, and the lover is sentenced to death. Isn't that algebra? Or another woman: she shoots herself in front of her husband but manages to whisper to the detective that it wasn't she but he who pulled the trigger, in order to get rid of her. Again there's a little something and they pack him off to hard labour. And now it doesn't matter whether she dies or pulls through. What matters is that there are things in this world that are worth paying a real price for.

It was fortunate that reading made the time and boredom pass more easily. Tania lay there daydreaming, turning over idle thoughts of how precise and unerring she could be in doing that very thing: shooting herself. Shooting herself – because the idea of 'pleasure' hadn't worked out: her roots were turning grey; Bologovsky was poor, tedious and old; and there was no one and nothing else to look forward to. She lay there on her back, her cold bare feet dangling, her arms flung back over her head, her hairless armpits exposed. But whose fault was it? Who could she blame? Ah, but wasn't it all the same? She wasn't interested in being just. Only she couldn't risk it. Maybe the detective — who would be willing to hear out her dying lie — wouldn't show up. (And it was unlikely that a priest would be around. Although it would be nice to lie once and for all in her dying confession.) No, she couldn't risk it. She would set it all up her own way. She would settle Bologovsky's fate, as a mother does for her child.

Enough for today. She got dressed (underwear that was full of holes and an old red dress which for some reason he liked) and went out to see Gulia. Again there had been a change. Now Gulia was taking a rich little girl out for her morning walk, for which Gulia received a few francs and lunch.

The kitten had grown up piebald. It scratched, walked on the table, and slept on Gulia's pillow. The whole room stank of him, an acrid, nauseating smell, rather than of Gulia's sharp perfume, which reminded Tania of methylated spirits.

Gulia's pale cheeks, her once beautiful face, which was now puffy and sickly, rested on her large open hands. Under her low forehead were two huge bovine eyes. Her knees were spread wide, and her two fat large feet in battered slippers loomed before Tania like two inanimate, inert objects. Gulia held a cheap cigarette holder with a dead butt in her long plump fingers. Her voice was deep, almost masculine.

'Today a flunkey, tomorrow kicked out. Then he can whistle for it. He'll be out of work. You've got to be tough.'

'He's jealous of every dog that comes along.'

'He's right in his own way. You wouldn't turn any dog down.'

Tania laughed knowingly. That meant Gulia considered her a '*grande amoureuse*'. Once they had talked about how Nadia and Tata weren't '*grandes amoureuses*'. Tania liked that.

'He hasn't any money, but he can play Mr Philosopher. Anyway, he's a little old for me, you know.'

'You don't say! That good-for-nothing. And he lets himself be jealous!'

Tania lit a cigarette. 'Yesterday he said to me: "I'll marry you or I'll kill you." '

'Why?'

'Oh, just like that. Out of hysteria.'

Gulia shifted her feet.

' "What" – he asks me – "are we all living for, you and me, everybody?" '

'But who does he think he is – Tolstoy or something? Tell him he's living so he can receive tips.'

Once again Tania burst out laughing.

'But what if,' she asked through her laughter, unable to tear her eyes from Gulia's legs, 'what if he really does slit my throat?'

'Why would he do a thing like that?'

'Does there have to be a reason for everything? Because he's bored.'

Then they started talking about other things: about how they could transform last year's hat, about Nadia, about Gulia's drunken lover, about the one really reliable form of birth control . . . It was getting dark. It was raining. From Gulia's tiny window you could see the intersection of two bluish-purple streets. The tram stop projected a raspberry-coloured star into the air, and the pavement was so wet that you couldn't tell up from down.

The days passed as if someone were dealing them out like cards, the same cards that Ella Martynovna once told Tania's fortune with and that Tania and Gulia played with now and then when there was nothing left to talk about. Tuesday, Wednesday, and another week gone by. And another. Again a Thursday. And it was already Saturday.

Once more the tram stop's raspberry star receded in the distance as Tania walked out of the building. When she arrived home she felt like shouting out, 'This has already happened before!' She turned on the light to wait for Bologovsky. He bored her, but she was even more bored by herself. 'Tasenka mine,' he said sometimes. 'Mine, mine, mine. It was God who sent you to me. Tell me, my dearest, wasn't it lucky that you came into our restaurant that time? Oh, you do love to eat well! Your last money – and scraped together from embroidering at that – and you throw it away on turkey. Just wait, my precious, this month I'm definitely going to get you some caviar, some real black grain caviar.'

She creased her eyes with pleasure. He kissed her and went behind the screens to undress. His stories started – who had ordered what and how much they had left behind. She listened, listened, and then fell asleep without washing. He was afraid to wake her up and so lay down cautiously beside her. The room was stuffy and full of cigarette smoke. It smelled of her, this woman, his woman. He had a woman. How wonderful it was and how terrifying. He had to write to his daughter to tell her that he was planning to get married. He hadn't told Tania that his daughter had a son, that he had a grandson, who was four. Wouldn't she be surprised! How were they doing there? Who cared though. The main thing was her. Not to wake her up.

Slowly (but his neck vertebrae cracked) he turned towards her and saw a glint in her face, the same glint that was reflected in the wash basin and the cupboard latch: it was a reflection of light, probably from the window. Her eyes were open, and she was looking past him. 'Tasenka,' he murmured, terrified of he didn't know what. She didn't respond, and that terrified him even more. He gripped her shoulder hard; it was warm, alive. 'What's wrong?'

'In. . .som. . .nia,' she muttered deliberately, her teeth set, with such hardness that it was as if someone else had said it.

He became quiet, and all his being listened. She was breathing. Wasn't she going to say something? Wasn't she going to make a move towards him?

'Have you ever thought about what my life is like?' she asked, and placed both hands on her breasts. 'Have you ever thought about what all this is for?'

He felt an inner shiver, an ache between his

throat and his heart, and a momentary deafness caused by his agitation. In a few seconds he would be able to hear her voice again.

' . . . unbearable. Do you understand? Unbearable. That time when I bought lobster and mayonnaise, I should have bought a gun instead. You saw the dressing gown with the tassels hanging there and you didn't even ask. You just thought: her husband. It's so boring! Let me go, for the love of Christ.'

He sat up on the bed, and in the darkness she saw his hands feeling his long head and then saw his narrow sloping shoulders become still again.

'I'm not holding you back. Wait, no, I am. I'm holding on to you. You're my last treasure. I already have a grandson, Volodia, Lidia's son. Where am I to . . . Tasenka? What am I supposed to do for you? What do you want? Maybe you'd like a child? You know, every woman . . . '

She raised her heavy body, and she too sat up, next to him. For a minute she couldn't get out a single word. Then she collapsed into tears and sobs and said:

'I'm talking about myself. What do you mean! I do everything to make sure there won't be one, and you ask. Good God, not to understand even that! Gulia would be laughing at me.'

Her tears, the darkness and stuffiness, and the patches of light jumped like fireflies from one object to another – but the main thing was her tears, which churned up everything inside him that was still unclouded. He switched on the light.

'What's the matter with you? What? Tasenka . . . '

But her tears had made her lose her train of thought. She could no longer remember how the conversation, this weeping, had started, or why. Was this what she'd been dreaming of all those years? Someone by her side who was prepared to love her and care for her all her life, so that she could lie around all day long without it mattering, remaking old dresses, shuffling cards? But revulsion for herself and for him as well had broken her spirit. She didn't know what life was, but she had a sense that this was not it. The years were slipping away from her. Now, with those oppressive thoughts, this tedium in her heart, her ageing breasts and sour face, where was she to go? Who would take her in hand and show her what to do? It was impossible that everything in the world could be this wretched, this bitter.

'I won't let you go. I love you, and I'm going to keep you. I'm holding on to you.' He repeated this. The light burned in the ceiling. His shoulders sloped, and his coarse grey chest appeared through the slit in his shirt.

'Turn out the light,' she said quietly. 'It's time to go to sleep.'

And, indeed, she soon fell asleep.

The night was long and flowed like a silent, endless river that seemed never to have had a beginning. For the first time in all these months of living with Tania, Bologovsky, downcast and filled with worry, recalled his former life, and suddenly he doubted that she could make him happy. He knew that in his memories everything fell into more or less the same order as it did for everyone else: the purity of childhood and the mistakes of youth; the burden of his fate in connection with his motherland; the loss of home, family; his wife's death; his daughter's marriage. Ten years working as a waiter. Two, no, three women in that time: one middle-aged relative; his dead wife's girlfriend, whom they had wanted him to marry; and a Frenchwoman he met on the boulevard on New Year's Eve. Which one? '32? '34?

He was drinking then . . . it had not been a happy period in his life, though it was the same for everyone, of course. He bet on the horses and drank. His daughter sent him money for a ticket and he drank that up as well. Then it passed, and a weariness set in that sometimes kept him from falling asleep at night and broke his back and shoulders. Especially that staggering around with the plates. Nonetheless, many people envied him.

And then she had appeared. Actually, he could hardly remember that memorable evening. She was sitting at a table stirring her coffee. Then they were sitting opposite one another, and there was a paper tulip, which also reminded him of his childhood. Later she turned out to have a white spot under her left breast, a scar from a childhood abscess, and two tender but sturdy tendons under her soft strong knee. So it was that then? Was that what all those years were for? Those and the others. Everything had come full circle; everything had been restored to him, maybe even more than had been promised.

Fear, sadness. What for? She was lying next to him, she was dreaming, and he was remembering, worried and sad, remembering his life without her. And when mentally he flung a bridge across that night, which coursed like a river, a bridge from the past into the future, he could not see Tania next to him. Once again he saw only himself, utterly alone, even more alone than before. Why? Probably because he had no imagination.

Morning, again morning, yet another morning, and yesterday's was gone. Maybe it hadn't happened at all. Maybe it was all the same morning repeating itself over and over and over again. The chipped blue coffee pot shuddered on the spirit lamp, and through the open window Tania could hear the swallows twittering as if it were spring. One thought, the same thought, took Tania's breath away. One sole thought.

When Bologovsky had moved in with her and brought over his two old trunks, she had hardly so much as glanced into his things, disdaining that old ragheap, his relics and old clothes, even a greasy volume of Kuprin. But at the time she did catch a glimpse in the rags of a very useful item (even then!), and she decided to confirm that that was what it was.

'Well, I'll be going now,' he said, like the tick of a pendulum. As soon as his steps died away she opened the first trunk, but there was nothing in it apart from some old and very dirty starched collars. The second was nearly full though. Tania sat down on a chair, tying a scarf over her housecoat, and plunged her head and arms under the lid.

What didn't he have there! Old suspenders and a few dozen razor blades, all rusty and black; empty cartridges; an oil lamp without its shade; pencils, rags, and a pile of brightly-coloured socks with holes you could put a fist through; used church tapers; a metre and a half of yellow and black ribbon for Saint George Crosses; a box that held an officer's cross wrapped in tissue paper; a piece of nice thick paper with gold seals on it that was disintegrating at the folds; letters scattered in and among the socks. In the bottom corner — the object she thought she'd seen (now she remembered him telling her at the time: 'It's not mine, no, but it does shoot quite well.') wrapped in a piece of a Bukhara silk shawl (blue and yellow paisleys along a dark red border), a small, heavy, long-since Russified Browning, its muzzle aimed at the corner of the trunk.

She picked it up as it was, in the shawl, but the shawl was so gaudy that she wrapped it all up together in a newspaper, yesterday's, which she had already devoured. And as she slipped the packet under her sheets she thought it was already starting to resemble one of the stories she'd read the day before, the one with the picture . . .

She had a plan. Like a military commander, like a traveller or a criminal, she had her very own plan. She had thought it up over the last few days while at home alone, and not just her brain but her whole being was consumed with it. Thinking about it made her thirsty, so she got up and walked over to the washstand and drank straight from the tap. The next thing was to take two precautionary measures: write a letter, one little letter, it didn't matter who to – it might as well be Belova, who was thorough and was likely to hold on to it; and go and see Gulia for one last time and say: I have this feeling, I'm scared.

No, there was a third thing as well, maybe the most important: warn the hotel concierge, get her worrying. 'Oh, Inspector, right then I thought: he's going to kill that woman, the brute. She looked at me so sweetly when she said: "Yes, we're definitely going to see that film tomorrow evening." (We have a cinema across the street, Inspector. We go there once a week, and so do all our lodgers.) "We're definitely going," that poor Russian lady said, "if we live that long."'

But why, what did she have to live for? What did Lila, her sister, live for, all dried up in her export office, or her father, rotting away paralysed? Had the land where she had married, where she had lived with Alexei Ivanovich, and where she had betrayed him, ever really existed? Nothing had happened in those years that was worth regretting, or worth loving. It always seemed to her that things could have been better, that they would get better, that others had it richer, happier, and fuller – what they call happiness. And even before that, in her childhood, in another country which she had long since forgotten. Ruses that were not completely innocent, a tortuous vanity, and, since she was nine, obscene dreams. It wasn't worth thinking about. Six feet under! Six feet under! To get out of here as fast as possible, having taken her revenge out on someone, anyone, revenge for her whole life all at once, having taken her revenge out on Bologovsky because the rest were all gone, scattered, hiding, the bastards.

He didn't give her much money, not because he was mean but because he didn't have it. When he lived alone he always had money, enough for himself, and once in a while there was even a hundred or two left over, which he sent to his daughter. Now things were tight sometimes, but nevertheless, as he rode home in the close air of the Metro surrounded by a wall of strange bodies and the smell of human breathing, he thought how he had something in common with that couple hugging in the corner, drunk with joy. Dark, stuffy stations went by. Sometimes he would notice a hunchbacked, grey-haired beggarwoman sitting on a bench carrying a cane and a brown bag, or an armless worker chewing on some bread, neither of them paying the slightest attention to the passing trains. Sometimes then strange thoughts would occur to Bologovsky, fear of some end, old age maybe, and the future loomed like a weight that he couldn't budge.

More and more insistently, more and more obstinately, not realising it himself, he was waiting for love to help him. He couldn't have said precisely what it was he required from that woman. Probably if asked he would have replied that he was completely content. But without putting it into words, in his heart, he was waiting for warmth, more warmth, a kind word, an understanding move in his direction, and maybe even . . . embroidery, which was how he imagined she had got by before she'd met him. Something to alleviate all that exhausting joy, in essence so much like a constant torment, which he kept skimming like foam off his trembling bliss – with kisses, with words, with his muffled laughter.

'Maybe,' he thought (these thoughts usually began as he was walking towards her hotel), 'maybe she had someone after her husband. After all, it's been five or six years since then. In the old days I wouldn't have dared think such a thing, but now everything's changed so much. She was living alone, and it was hard on her. Oh, so what! What do I care? But what if she's deceiving me now? No, that's ridiculous.'

He himself was neither jealous nor suspicious, but he needed his daily ration of torment or reassurance, and it was precisely that which was missing. Every time he reached the front door, on the very threshold, the worry that there, inside, things had changed pressed on his heart; he was afraid to think that everything had gone cold up there, that there was nothing up there at all. Then as the door slammed shut he would run up the stairs on his thin legs, three steps at a time, simply to convince himself that Tania still existed.

She was sitting on a chair in the middle of the room completely undressed, waiting for the ten red nails on her hands and the ten on her feet to dry. She was very white, and her large round stomach and belly changed shape depending on how she sat. There was practically no hair on her body – her lack of eyebrows gave a hint of that. She had her legs stretched out in front of her and her arms hanging by her sides, and she was waiting. Her face wore the expression, resigned and obtuse, that she herself never saw but which others did.

'Someone's been here,' he said, sensing a presence in the air. The ashtray was full of butts.

'Gulia,' she responded, not stirring.

'What's wrong with her?'

'She got worried so she dropped in.'

He started to undress.

'What was she worried about?'

'Me. How you and I are getting along.'

He took off his coat, hat and jacket and tugged his feet, stiff with exhaustion, out of his shoes. He sat down at the table and started looking at her, naked and still, at her heavy breasts, at her twenty nails as red as radishes.

'So it's you? The same old you?' he asked

himself cautiously. 'Lord, but who are you? Why are you so naked? Cover yourself, for God's sake. I beg you!' He said this to himself, and at the same time he felt that he was losing the gift of speech, as if his voice and tongue were being taken away from him. 'Keep quiet. Better keep quiet.' Suddenly he made a strange face as if his mouth had been slit with a razor and then pressed together. Bologovsky stretched his hairy arms across the table and waited for this woman to get up and cover her nakedness.

Finally she got up, found her slippers, and started dressing two steps from him. It was strange for him to have her so close, so accessible, and to have no desire even to watch her.

'Gulia's worried about me and so is Belova. Even the concierge downstairs says "*Dieu merci*" every time she sees me. I can tell by their faces that if I croaked after eating mushrooms or rotten fish they'd suspect you of poisoning me,' she chuckled, tugging at her soiled, purplish-pink girdle. 'Well, why don't you say something? Just you wait. I'll die and then you'll find out. Talk! Oh, I'm so fed up with it all, fed up. Everything's old and worn out.' She hitched her brassière with a safety pin. 'My hair's a mess, and my powder's almost run out. Say something!' And she froze, in one stocking, looking at Bologovsky with hatred. 'If you're going to live with me, then talk! Why do you go on living? Why do you go on living at all? Do you hear what I'm asking you or not?' she yelled, sobbing.

He moved his fingers but said nothing, a shiver passed across his face, and his eyes grew even more metallic.

'And I thought I could live with a man like that somehow . . . somehow,' she muttered, grabbing her hair with both hands in anguish. 'Do you understand that I feel nothing for you but hatred? Nothing! Why have you been feeding me for three months? Why have you been sleeping with me? Watch, I'll shoot myself right now, and the police will arrest you. And just before I do I'll ring the bell. I'll scream . . . '

She jumped up, but he jumped up too and barred the way.

Where was she running to? Not to him. Not to the bell, which was at the head of the bed. To the cupboard. He was still unable to overcome his muteness, and couldn't utter a word. What kind of words did he have anyway? Tenderness? Anger? She had stopped by the cupboard doors, half-dressed and holding a stocking in her hand. While he quickly slipped his feet into the shoes tossed under the table, while he pulled on his jacket and coat – still mute – she remained by the cupboard, apparently lacking the nerve to go through with what she had intended. Her face was frightening now; another four, three . . . two seconds . . . no, she couldn't do what had seemed so simple and easy before. One second. Not even unwrapping the Bukhara shawl, if she could only reach the bell; through the shawl into my stomach, into my soft warm stomach, sending the shot and my scream all through the building. (By that time he was running down the stairs.) 'What happened?' 'She's shot herself,' he tells the people running towards him. 'See, she's still holding the gun.' 'Not on your life, you're under arrest,' they reply. 'If she'd shot herself she wouldn't have rung the bell. She wouldn't have called out for help. She wouldn't have made every other person all this past week think she was afraid of you. You killed her.' 'But I ran out onto the stairs *before* the shot. Ask the neighbours.' And then someone will say (under oath) that first there came the shot and then the steps on the landing, and another someone (also under oath) that first there came the steps and then the shot.

He was already far away, out on the street, and she was still standing next to the cupboard, stock-still. Instead of thinking about what in fact had kept her from carrying out what she had intended, she thought about trivial things: what time could it be? Look at that cobweb hanging from the ceiling. What was that over there? What is this kind of mental illness called? Mania. Some kind of mania. Lympho . . . lymphomania. No, what am I saying! Mythomania. From the word 'myth'. I dreamed up a story which you could get money for from one of those newspapers if you wrote it down. I dreamed up . . . My God, where is he? My God, he's run out on me!

Six o'clock. A green-shaded lamp is lit near the cashier's dish. Seven men in identical white jackets are soundlessly setting the tables. The trolley, with a rustling noise, brings hors d'oeuvres and the tarte maison topped with cream up from the refrigerator. Someone wipes glasses and carries them stem up. Bologovsky moves back and forth in the aquarium light, sorting silver forks. At seven fifteen the front door starts swinging: the first customers walk in; others follow. First places are taken in the four corners of the room;

then in the middle. The light burns. Voices. Hot bowls sail past, an ice bucket for one table, *shashlik* brought in on long skewers. The room fills up. Eight o'clock. There isn't a single free table. Fortissimo sounds from the invisible orchestra and then a gradual quieting of voices and movements, an ebb of people, plates, and glasses (stem down); the gathering of napkins, the stacking of chairs; one lamp goes out, another, a third. The clock says ten, ten on the dot. Outside is a spring night, a May night. Paris hasn't changed. It is hard to believe somehow.

He walked along, thinking, but his thoughts did not come easily. All he felt was disgust at her nakedness and her tears. As he went over in his mind the three months he had lived with her everything, or nearly everything, took on that aspect – cynical, insulting, false. There was nothing you could grab hold of; it was all so slippery, so vile. And hardest of all to bear was the awareness of his own vain self-deception. In that respect she was not herself, nor was he himself.

He walked the streets through the gloom and damp of the evening, taking no notice of passers-by. At the lights he stopped in for a drink, and the alcohol helped his soul – yes, here was proof of its existence – stretch its dusty wings. To let change jangle on zinc one last time, to take a swig and feel the warmth run down his shoulders and ribs, the very warmth he had had so little of. Here was another corner, a streetlamp, a chemist. There was a big muddy ice wagon; there was a horse. Don't get confused please. What does artillery have to do with it? The Nikolaevsky Cavalry, a great institution . . .

'Oh, go on with you,' he says, pushing his hat back on his head and putting his arms around the docile, big-eyed light chestnut's muzzle. 'Oh, go on with you.'

He strokes it, tousles its mane, kisses it on the lips, and sniffs the air blowing in his face from its docile nostrils. And it sniffs him back so that they're both sniffing each other.

'Oh, go on with you, you recognised me. You remembered,' Bologovsky says. 'You haven't forgotten.' He rubs his cheek, his cheek and his whole face, against the horse and strokes it with both hands.

The iceman comes back from delivering a block of ice to the café, silently crawls into his box, silently lifts his whip. And the horse walks away, indifferent, submissive, leaving Bologovsky alone.

When he flung the door open and entered, Tania was standing in the dark pressed up against the wall, kneading her hands and clutching an end of the Bukhara shawl to her breast. (Where had he seen that shawl, and when?)

'Tasenka, what's the matter with you? Anyone would think you were trying to scare me,' he said and smiled.

She moved away from him, mistrustful.

'Where have you been?'

'What do you mean, where have I been? I've been working. I'm a waiter, remember?'

He reeked of wine, and his hat was crushed to one side.

'Tasenka, tell me . . .'

She clutched the bit of shawl tightly to her breast. He came towards her, and a depth she didn't know opened up in his eyes.

'So tell me, you don't love me? "In a sort of way" you say. I don't think it's a "sort of way", but in a very particular way, so particular that it's frightening to say out loud.'

He stood close to her, put his hands on her shoulders, and pressed his chest against hers.

'So there wasn't any point to it after all, eh? Come on, sweetheart, how many were there before me?'

She didn't respond. The gun was poking into her chest and his too, but he hadn't noticed it.

'Tell me how many there were and I'll let you go. You'll be free, the way you were before. Damn you, little idiot! It didn't work out. Forget it!'

'You're running out on me?' she whispered, frightened, and tried to reach the trigger under the silk. Suddenly he moved back and grabbed the muzzle with his right hand.

'What the hell is this?' he asked, sobering up a little. She began to fall back slowly. 'No, don't you faint. You're a good actress, I should know. I know how well . . . So what on earth is this?' She stopped her fall and leaned against the wall, breathing heavily. Her face was frozen, white, wet. He gripped her wrist with one hand and twirled the Browning in the other, holding it by the muzzle, and the shawl fluttered like a flag. 'What on earth is this? What is it?' he spluttered. Letting the gun drop to the floor with a thud, he grabbed her arms with both hands now and, digging his fingers into their fleshiness, panting, forced her to bend and jerked her away from the door.

'I'll scream,' she cried, bumping her head on the headboard and watching to see he didn't pick the weapon up again.

'Kill? Me? She wanted to kill me!' he whispered, making her bend over even further, dragging her, pulling her, shaking her so hard that she finally gasped and fell between the bed and the table.

'Let me go,' she wailed. She struggled, like a big fish, squirming to get out from under him, feeling his familiar heavy body on top of her. He crushed her with his knees and chest, pressing, breaking her arms: 'Why did you do it, you viper? Why?' he muttered. His whole face – so close to hers – was covered with a grid of swollen veins.

'I was joking, joking, jo-king,' she repeated senselessly, still trying to throw him off, knocking her head on something hard in the process. He turned her face towards him with his elbow, crushed her arms even tighter with his chest and left arm, and with his right grabbed her by her velvety white throat, which felt so much like the place behind her knee that he touched sometimes, above the calf: two firm tendons and that soft skin, strength and weakness.

'A-a-ah,' she wailed, and her two terrified and dulled blue eyes bulged. 'A-a-ah!' But the second time it came out as a rasp, not a wail.

Yes, those same two firm, sturdy tendons, he realised soberly, something round in the middle and all wrapped in quivering lard, into which he dug his hairy fingers. He squeezed it for a long time until it stopped throbbing. Was she really dead? What if she were still alive? He grabbed a pillow from the bed and threw it on her face, threw another on her chest, and lay down again, crushing her, unable to believe she wouldn't come round.

There was a loud crash against the door. Wait . . . I'd better make sure there aren't any gaps. Otherwise – it would be too frightening if she turned out to be alive, with those nails, those moans and those spasms, that past he didn't know, that future . . . But, thank God, there was no future.

Astashev in Paris

I

Mamma lived on the seventh floor of a very large old building. The entire floor was rented out by the room; people ate, slept, and cooked in each room, and in the evening they took their rubbish bins out to a common hallway. The old-fashioned hydraulic lift broke down every other day. The stairwell, which had no windows, was not always lit, and the cast-iron door to the street was too heavy, and that was why Mamma almost never went out. A neighbour ran to the shop for her, and Mamma only visited either on her own floor or one flight down – the building had been taken over by Russians. She only went downstairs to go to church, and then only for the main holy days. Afterwards, getting back up, using her umbrella like a cane, took so long and made her so short of breath that she was nearly reduced to tears. When she met friends at the candle box and they said, 'You must drop in for a cup of tea sometime, Klavdia Ivanovna,' all she could think of was that lift, the lift, the unlit landings, and the steep, hollowed-out steps. 'You've got a home. Stay put.' That was how she saw it. 'Otherwise you'll go out one day and won't come back. You'll get stranded between floors or choke to death on the pavement.'

Indeed, Alyosha found his mother's apartment quite agreeably situated, as the higher up you were the fresher the air. When he came to visit he made sure the window was wide open. It looked onto a round window-less building that resembled a globe: the gas plant. Behind it you could see an endless murk of buildings, roofs, windows, and a tower that came in and out of view, sometimes with a flag, sometimes not, sometimes with its top cut off, sometimes with the statue of an angel on it.

'How lucky you are, Mamma,' Alyosha used to say. 'Such tranquillity, such peace of mind.' Then he sat down to drink tea and eat some pie, a pretzel, jam, to read the papers he had brought along with him. Or sometimes his eyes fixed absentmindedly on her trembl-ing head, her sparse hair, her dry hands and bent fingers. 'I've made it possible for you to live exactly as you please,' he used to say, 'and I live exactly as I please, too. You and I have already been through more than enough. *Assez*, now, *assez, assez*. You have electricity, a heated bathroom, sun – and curtains if you feel like shutting it out. Your central heating works, and your papers are in perfect order. All that is what's known as comfort, Mamma. Yes! And we both have it now because I . . . well, thank God.'

She sat at the table and nodded in agreement, smiling. She was knitting – without looking down – a thick white sweater for him. In front of her on the table lay a picture from a fashion magazine showing a young man with a long tanned face wearing a thick white sweater and sticking his chest out. She looked at it as she knitted, counting to herself, and it was in fact coming out very much like the picture. The ball of white wool bobbed up and down on her knees. Alexei Georgievich kept opening and closing the windows, making sure that the bolts were working. He turned the light off and on, jumped to see whether the parquet creaked, and pulled at the curtains to make sure they were up securely.

'That lift of ours broke down again yesterday,' she said sadly. 'They were fixing something. They say something's broken in the basement. They never did fix it, though. Just gave up.'

But he didn't pay much attention to what she said. Either he talked or he read. When he was talking to her he never said a word about his business, about the people at the office. Instead he reminisced about things that had happened long ago, as you would with an old ally with whom you have no present in common but with whom you share a past – and what a past! It had been a long battle they would both remember and respect forever: she because her Alyosha was its hero, and he – for the same reason. Or else he told her about something unusual he had seen on the street. But the past, their common forty-year past, was much more real than their shabby and soulless present.

'Mamma, do you remember when we lived on Siverskaya? Remember I had a little navy blue suit that summer Papa went away and the silver was stolen? Remember what a plump, energetic little boy I was then? And my dream was to train porcupines and join the circus?'

She remembered of course.

'Today I was walking along, and what did I see? Children sailing toy boats on the pond in the square. Mamma, technology has even reached silly games like that. I felt upset. Why was it ordained from birth that I should have to make do with flat-bottom boats made of tree bark?'

His big blue eyes looked straight ahead as he recalled a Russian pond, willows, his fat knees, and his trousers rolled up. When did that end?

'Childhood stopped in a very abrupt way, Mamma. Was it after college? I always seemed to be marching off with a black knapsack slung over my shoulders. March, march, march! It's just as if I'd kept on marching right up till today. I'm still young. You used to give me thirty kopeks for lunch, and I spent twelve and saved eighteen. Then, when you sent me to Moscow – remember? – I saved masses of money on my hotel. Let me have a pencil.'

She nodded, crossed herself, and flicked away a tear from her old eyes.

'And now, Alyoshenka, and now!'

'It's even funny if you think of the money I saved. Yes, a lot has happened. But the main thing was having to start all over again from scratch here. You can't get away with just any old thing here, like you could back home. Here it takes something completely different. But I was born a European. It would have been simply ridiculous for me to live in Russia.'

'And yet . . . if I could take just one look at it!'

'People often say to me: "Astashev, are you really Russian? You're just like one of us."'

Later she hugged his pudgy, flabby body and his clean hands with their pink palms and delicate triangular fingernails, stroked his dark blue jacket and fair hair, and gazed into his round, youthful, baby-smooth face.

'My clever boy,' she said. 'My consolation.'

He kissed her, looked at his watch again, and since it was after eight, he left.

'Where are you going now?' she asked. 'Have you got yourself a sweetheart?'

He replied, while fastidiously buttoning his well-made coat:

'Mamma, I have no business having a sweetheart. Siring beggars is not my sort of thing. Sometimes I make an exception for the sake of my health, but I have to wait a minimum of three years to marry.'

'Well, may the Lord protect you,' she whispered.

She never did find out where he went. In all these years she never had the least idea.

Half an hour later he was ringing the bell at a broad polished door where the stairs were carpeted and palms flanked the downstairs mirror.

'That must be Alexei,' said a woman's voice in the next room as the servant was helping him off with his coat.

'Yes, it's me, Mamenka,' he replied. 'Hello.'

'Hello there, vulture. Whose bones did you pick clean today?'

He walked over to where she was sitting, clicked his heels, and kissed her hand. Usually there was someone else there, and Xenia Andreevna's behaviour with him was playfully haughty.

'Did you hear? "*Mamenka*!"' she exclaimed. But her dyed red hair, sagging bust, and the thick layer of powder on her neck betrayed her age ruthlessly. 'You make me feel old, you gangster!'

This was Alyosha's father's second wife, his stepmother, who once won a great victory over Klavdia Ivanovna.

He bloomed there like a rare and special flower. He made himself comfortable in an armchair, made endless witty remarks, laughed loudly and gazed unctuously at Xenia

Andreevna and at her guests – officials, well-off, whom Mamenka was encouraging. Despite the difference in ages, Alyosha could keep up with their idiosyncratic conversation: stories of deputies, chairmen, and vice-chairmen, of elections for some committee, or committee council, or council executive. Evgraf Evgrafovich hinted at the possible candidacy of Yuli Fyodorovich to the audit commission. One guest gave a significant look; another guest felt that a recount was inevitable; and Mamenka intrigued venomously and opportunistically on behalf of Admiral Vyazminitinov, who had made someone a charitable donation.

Alexei Georgievich suddenly asked for champagne, told a funny story, kissed Xenia Andreevna's hands, and behaved like a spoiled child who can get away with anything. Then he became respectful and kind, produced a free theatre ticket from his pocket and offered it to all and sundry present, and took his leave.

Alexei Georgievich had lived with his father for one half of his life, and the other half with his mother; a month here, a week there; a winter here, a summer there. He was ten when his father had walked out on the family, moved in with a woman who called herself an actress, and continued to support his wife and the two children, he and his sister Nyuta, haphazardly and meagrely. Nyuta died a year later of meningitis. He went to one of the modern high schools. They lived on Pesk, in a dingy apartment with one entrance that was furnished with their bulky and nondescript furniture. There were small windows between the rooms to let in more light, and fat spiders spun their webs up by the ceilings. His mother and nurse, who were preoccupied with cleaning the painted floors and starching the curtains, never knocked them down. Sometimes in the evenings, engulfed in their own brocade and protected by female superstition, the spiders ran out to the middle of the ceiling, fell on one another, and sucked each other dry, whereupon they shrivelled up and fell to the floor.

When he came home from school, Alexei went straight to his desk in a room full of trunks and cupboards, where the window vent stayed closed for weeks on end. He sat like that until nightfall, writing compositions, solving problems, looking a chapter ahead in history and Russian to get an idea about the next day's lesson. There was a walnut shelf over his desk where he kept his Latin texts, mimeographed solutions to theorems, *Sample Compositions for the Sixth, Seventh and Eighth Classes, Teach Yourself Physics,* and *Geography Exam Questions with Their Answers.* He only had to have one textbook per subject, but he had several: Sipovsky, Savodnik, Nezelenov, Smirnovsky, Kraievich and Zinger, Lebedev, Smirnov, and Yanchev, Kiselev and Davydov, and for history Illovaisky, Platonov, Vinogradov, Belyarminov, Elpatievsky, and someone else whose name he didn't know because the title page had been torn out. Alexei Georgievich had acquired all these textbooks through exchange: he took his mother's books – Pushkin, Lermontov, Mamin-Sibiryak, Sheller-Mikhailov, and sometimes Zola's novels in translation – out of their narrow, glass-doored, silk-curtained bookcase and swapped them at school (they all knew him there) for textbooks, which students in all grades passed on to him – not just theirs but their older brothers' and sisters' as well.

He was at the top of his class. He sat right under the teacher's nose in the first row. For a very long time he was shorter than everyone else, and since his last name began with an A, he was all the more visible. Everything started with him: the two-by-two procession, examinations, question-and-answer periods.

He always recited whatever greeting was called for, and it was he who always answered the inspector's questions as well. Cleaning the blackboard was his job, and so was the chalk, for some reason. And despite all this no one ever took it into their head to be jealous of him.

On Saturdays Alyosha didn't go home after school. Instead he took the no. 14 tram to Sennaya Street. A year before his father had been disbarred for some rather less than honest dealings, and now he was 'in business'. The apartment was quite pleasant, with a gilded frieze in the foyer and velvet and leather and even a servant – a grubby, pimply boy with greasy hair and a drinker's nose. Alyosha had the utmost respect for his father and his father's servant, apartment, and new wife. Here was a real woman, the first woman he'd had a chance to study at close hand – dressed, half-dressed, undressed, in sickness and in health. Here was a real woman, who bore some inexplicable relationship to his father's wallet. In her vicinity Alyosha always felt a little anxious, giddy, and not altogether comfortable.

He stayed there until Monday morning. His life for those two days bore no resemblance to life with Klavdia Ivanovna. Saturday was Mamenka's *jour fixe*: guests sat in the drawing room drinking tea, making witty remarks, and gossiping. And he would put his homework off until later, until that night, and sit in an armchair, his eyes bulging, unable to tear himself away, mentally unbuttoning the women's gathered silk dresses, mentally crawling into the men's shoes and swallowing whole the éclairs, Napoleons, cream puffs and bouchées, and all their words and puns, which showered down like peas, like shot, like pearls.

They were three at the evening meal: Papa, bald, with thick eyebrows and a handlebar moustache, looking like something off the cover of a gypsy romance; Mamenka, Xenia Andreevna, wearing a transparent robe with flowing sleeves; and Alexei. Sometimes after supper his father and stepmother drove to the theatre, and he lounged about the apartment for a long time examining the contents of drawers – both locked and unlocked – and then sat down to his homework. Sometimes they took him with them to the theatre – operetta, farce, Suvorin. Once, one Sunday afternoon, they took him to see *The Government Inspector* because he had studied Gogol recently at school.

Usually on Sunday, though, he got up late

and read the newspapers from cover to cover over tea, like a novel, from the front-page obituaries to the personal columns at the back. After breakfast Xenia Andreevna took him for a walk. They walked down Nevsky and Sadovaya to the Summer Garden, where they ran into people they knew.

'Oh, my God! Whose young man is this?'

'This is my son,' she would say. 'Isn't it odd that I should have such a grown-up son?'

The bewildered listener would smile in silence.

'Doesn't he look like me?'

And when the whole thing was cleared up there would be lots of laughter, lots of teasing on her part, and lots of feeble jokes on the other's.

Drifting off to sleep at night, Alexei Georgievich used to hear his father quarrelling with Xenia Andreevna, things breaking − a pitcher, a perfume bottle − a chair falling, their whispers and shouts becoming less and less constrained, less and less self-conscious. In the morning he never saw anyone. The servant brought him his glass of tea, and he ate a roll and walked his quick, rolling walk to the tram stop. During the winter the street-lamps were still burning through the snow and fog. Cutting through the gloom,

the tram car rolled along, jingling its bell, and
Alyosha sat and looked at the old ladies, at
the women, at the fine ladies swathed in fox
and sable, and found that there was something which attracted him in nearly all of
them.

On Monday he went back home after
school. Klavdia Ivanovna latched on to his
overcoat, his nurse came out of the kitchen,
and they both set about tormenting him.
What did he have to eat? Didn't he starve?
Didn't he catch a chill? Didn't anyone insult
him? He fended them off, saying as he walked
away: 'It's always the same, tiresome really.
Xenia Andreevna ordered herself a new fur
coat with fox tails. I think Papa is going to get
himself horses.'

Having driven this nail into the maternal
heart, he went to do his maths, nestling his
round chin (on which nothing would grow
for a long time) in the soft bed of his hand.
This studying, this effort, this sweat, went on
all week until the weekend came around once
more, like an unexpected and illicit flourish
on a plain government building.

He was blue-eyed, quiet, and combined
when necessary both speed (serving and
fetching) and dependability. His face was
pale and serious, and his disposition excel-

lent. He never got particularly close to anyone, never played darts or cards, and never lent money. He was growing up, and it was gradually becoming clear that he hadn't read anything apart from his textbooks. On the other hand, he knew what he needed to know by heart. When he turned sixteen he heard a conversation about women. The conversation was eminently pragmatic and dry, more as if it were a matter of choosing a subject to read at University or an obligatory Lenten fast. It was one of those Saturdays. In the evening he was at his father's, having mapped out his plan of action. Late that night, when everyone was asleep, he pulled his trousers on and went barefoot to the cook, a young, still attractive, furtive woman, and within half an hour he was back in his room. In that half-hour he had not opened his mouth or uttered a word, so that finally the cook had said to him: 'But why, Alyoshenka? Why don't you say something? You're so quiet for such a young man.'

At twenty he lost his father. At the time Xenia Andreevna was in Kislovodsk, where she hobnobbed with White generals, with second lieutenants, wore white lace shirts, and composed and published a patriotic novel. Alyosha stayed in Petersburg with

Klavdia Ivanovna, working in a Soviet institution, going hungry. In his humiliated thoughts he cherished proud Bonapartist plans without even being able to give them a name. It was during those years that his savage hatred for authority, for the people, for his country, was born. No prince of the blood or old-line nobleman could have contemplated the goings-on in Russia with the same rage and shiver as Alyosha.

He hated all of it: the vast expanses, which themselves could lead to ruin due to the impossibility of keeping a people who cracked sunflower seeds in their teeth and blew their noses into their hand under police control all the way to the trackless frontiers; the disorder of history, right up to the succession after Peter the First, which he perceived as an unforgivable blunder, from which he was now forced to extricate himself. He hated the entire nineteenth century, which seemed like an apocalyptic sign, each decade speaking of the future in the accursed tongue of prophecy. He liked to recall the last four lost wars and the tattered, unkempt 'vanguard', which had been half infiltrated with police agents, who joined them in tossing bombs.

When the borders opened up in 1925 and

he found himself in Paris he used to refer to Russia as the Soviet Republic, the Bolsheviks as the comrades, and Lenin as the German spy. He believed that he had miraculously escaped execution and used to say that they were raising fourteen-year-olds of unknown patrimony at the state's expense and that the peasants were eating human flesh. Then that passed and he forgot all about Russia. A new life began in a new place. And at first he had such a life-and-death struggle with it that he nearly gave up.

The two of them were living in the suburbs in an unheated room. Klavdia Ivanovna went out to iron during the day. He watched this relatively young, strong woman being transformed into an old woman who suffered from a hernia and had bleeding callouses on her overworked fingers. He ran all over town. What did he know how to do? What could he do? Work in an office, wash dishes in a restaurant, be a delivery boy in a Russian pastry shop, sell vacuum cleaners door to door? He did all those things until he finally grew numb from it all and got fed up with it, fed up with trembling over every penny he made. Had he been able to steal without getting caught he would have stolen, but he didn't have any idea of where or how business of that kind was carried out.

Even in that restless indigence, from one niggardly day to the next, he was being drawn in a specific direction and had made a definite choice, adamantly preferring selling for a commission – long hours and fruitless running from house to house and up and down stairs – to sitting in an office. They told him to find someone who would like to acquire a piano (or a sewing machine, or a radio, to say nothing of a bicycle, encyclopedia, or the latest model carpetsweeper), and he looked – but he never found anyone. He felt the stony damp cold of the pavement through his soles and the hundreds of steps in his heart, but he did not give up his vague hope that on that very pavement, on those very stairs, he would catch a glimpse of his prosperity.

Towards the end of the third winter, when Klavdia Ivanovna was taken to the hospital for an operation, he took advantage of the fact that she wouldn't be seeing the papers and placed an advertisement: Xenia Andreevna Astasheva – Please contact your son. A letter arrived at the office of the newspaper. Xenia Andreevna gave him her address, asked him to come to see her right away, and expressed her amazement that neither Nadezhda Petrovna, Vassily Vassilievich,

Zhenya Sokolova, nor the Sipatievs had told him that she was in Paris. He had never known these people.

She understood everything the moment he walked in, and although she was considerably changed (she had been forty, now she was fifty), he had changed even more. A kind of dark puffiness, a crushed look, had appeared in his face, and his voice was louder. It was as if Alyosha were in a state of constant indignation over something. His eyes had become furtive and lacklustre, and his mouth, pale and wet, had spread out across his face. He still didn't know whether he could – or should – tell her. He hitched his thumb in the armhole of his waistcoat and smoked the cigarette she offered him. He didn't know whether to launch into his story snorting and foaming. It was certainly a story beyond her wildest dreams.

'Well, my handsome blond,' she said in her deep voice, toying with the chain at her neck that he had known since childhood, 'tell me about it, don't be a fool.'

The room was not hers. She had rented it furnished, but it was an expensive room with red silk curtains and a grand piano. (She didn't need a vacuum cleaner, did she? No, probably not.) There were three bottles on the table – refreshments she planned to treat him to, although he felt like a veal chop, baked ham, beef, roasted or stewed beef.

'I'm lost here,' he said. He placed his unlit cigarette back on the table and looked down at his hands, at his bitten fingernails. 'Can't you think up something, Mamenka?'

She had him drink a small glass of Benedictine, which made him feel warm, and his thoughts became sweet and misty. Crossing one large elegant leg over the other, revealing a silken knee under her short slim skirt, she sat before him – not young and not old, her hair dyed, her veins prominent, self-assured – and smoked. She didn't smile. There was nothing to smile at.

'I'll give you a chance,' she said in her bass voice, giving him a penetrating look. 'Listen closely, my number one student. Just a moment and I'll get you something to eat. There's something left from lunch.'

She went out. Her perfume lingered in the air, strong heavy perfume. He looked around. Who was she? What was she? In the morning, for example, when she gets up, what does she do? Where does she go? Who pays for all of this?

She came back. Roast beef with mustard and bread. He ate it all. He drank another liqueur. Mustard and Benedictine. He liked it. He would have to do it again sometime, when he could afford it.

'Listen. First of all, about me. I have a Frenchman. God save the soul of Georgy Ivanovich' – she crossed herself deliberately – 'there'll never be anyone like him: talent, spirit, the old guard. But I don't have to tell you – you're his son. Remember one thing: he was an extraordinary man. But this Frenchman cropped up on a train, and it's been a fairy tale, a novel! He got hooked, like a trout on a line. He's been keeping me for over three years. Fantastically intelligent, magnificent blood, a musician. He was an expert advisor in affairs of state, but now he's retired. There's one drawback though: he's over seventy.'

'Oh, my God!' he sighed sympathetically.

'What are you gasping for? Think! That's not so much for a well-preserved man. After all, I'm not sixteen anymore. But there is still a danger. He nearly died of a heart attack this autumn. And there's a family, a wife, children. There's another mistress he's had for thirty years. And there's yet another actress, a horrible bitch, she sleeps with ministers. He needs her for business purposes, he meets useful people at her place. In short, I'm giving you a chance. Instead of going around trying to talk people into providing themselves with things they don't need – insure him, making me the beneficiary.'

'What did you say?' He didn't understand, but by her face he could tell she had come to the crucial point.

'Are you drunk? On one glass? I said: Go and make yourself an insurance agent. You'll meet him here and get friendly. Only no "Mamenka" when he's around. Use something vague, "*ma cousine*", for example, for that matter, on my husband's side, a distant relative . . . twice removed. He'll ask you: And what do you do, young man? You'll see, he's a true gentleman, he talks like a professor. You tell him about some real-life cases. Make him understand what it means to leave your loved ones beggars. Don't scare him off with death, no one likes that. But allude to the fifth act, to the last curtain that falls without warning.'

He laughed knowingly, by now completely drunk. He wasn't used to drinking.

'Oh, Mamenka, you're amazing! You're so good, so sweet, so clever! I'm going to kiss you. I'm definitely going to kiss you! You always seemed like perfection itself to me. At one time your peignoirs got me quite excited.

At least give me your hand, if that's the way you want it, like mother and son.'

'You idiot,' she said, flattered nonetheless.

All of a sudden he sobered up, pulled himself together, and coughed.

'But what if it doesn't work out? I mean, what I meant to say was, what if it does work out?'

'You'll get a percentage. If you get him up to half a million, that will mean a pretty penny.'

'But that's likely to cost him a small fortune, especially if he's getting old.'

'It will cost him a lot of money, but he's rich.'

Alyosha thought it over. He touched the glass and licked his sticky finger.

'But what then?'

'To start out all you need is the first fifty thousand francs,' she said simply. She drained her glass, her eyes half-closed.

He watched her and suddenly began to laugh again, but differently now – a moist, pensive laugh.

'It really would be nice, my dear Mamenka,' he mumbled, and something joyful shone in his face. 'Oh, it really would be nice! Is it possible? And in such an honest, such a good way? You know, Mamenka, I do like honesty. I'm not a rascal. I could never kill anyone, for instance. I couldn't even rob. I've never tried to seduce a married woman, I swear. I've always preferred unattached ones. I can't think of a single sin I've ever committed. So why should I suffer like this?' He fell silent, waiting for the tears under his eyelids to go away. 'My God, why? I don't have a bad disposition, I'm clean, polite, and if I don't recite poetry or go to concerts, that's no crime, after all.'

She listened to him ramble. The light was failing in the room. The long noses of the silk dolls on the sofa were drooping into the festoons of their colourful dresses. Then she stood up, switched on the light, powdered her face, put on a striking tall hat, and took him out to shop. She enjoyed the fact that he was young and decent-looking, that they were as close as ever, and that together they would follow through on an idea that had been obsessing her for over a year.

When he recalled now – which he did very rarely – that old man, who turned out to be sixty-nine (he found out his exact age when, in accordance with all the rules of the insurance game, he brought the doctor to examine him before the policy signing and first payment), when he now recalled that enchanting, silver-haired, frail old man, who when it was all over gave him a little notebook with a place for a pencil on the side and who proceeded, very shortly thereafter, to die, it seemed as if it had all happened long long ago, on the threshold between childhood and adulthood. And what a wretch he had been when he was so down and out that he was driven to placing that announcement in the paper and then brought Klavdia Ivanovna home from the hospital, back to their unheated room, so that she could start doing daywork again! But he didn't think about that very much, and gradually all of it – the meeting with Xenia Andreevna, the new shirts, '*ma cousine*', evening chess games with Monsieur Robert, turning pages for him when he did his relaxed, tender rendition of Schumann – all of it had grown so bent and twisted that now he found it offensive and ridiculous to dredge it up from his memory, where it slumbered. His life had changed so drastically. Things were moving along with such energy and smoothness, he was living so independently, with such confidence, that he even permitted himself little affairs now and then. He felt so on top of everything that once in a while he would whistle a popular foxtrot around his neatly kept, comfortable, bachelor apartment.

II

The morning was fresh and sparkling. The sun had already managed to break through twice, and twice it had poured with rain, lacquering the pavement. The sky was azure and black, and the wind made Alexei Georgievich's nostrils twitch like an animal's when he emerged wearing a bowler and carrying an umbrella and briefcase, set out down the street, and turned towards the bus stop. His face, which he had just washed, glowed, and there was a clarity and a blueness in his eyes. In fact, there was something about his entire appearance that corresponded to that morning, that hour, the air, the weather, something healthy, vigorous, intense, and restless.

Astashev had still not altogether adjusted to his new apartment, which he had moved into a month before. He changed his place of residence rather frequently and left without leaving a forwarding address. Usually his departures coincided with the end of an affair. 'A clean break', 'not striking the last chord' – as he referred to the liquidation of his relationships with women. Recently he found himself thinking more in French than Russian, and he already knew all kinds of appropriate expressions for this in French. At the same time they were much more in keeping with the actual essence of his affairs, since the objects of his affection tended more and more to be French – he did not care for Russian women.

His breath was a blend of strong coffee and Swiss mouthwash. He never smoked. In his head he had the address of a prominent businessman – his home address. Astashev tried not to go to offices. He hurried, as he was anxious to catch his client at home. His thoughts took their usual course. Early in the morning he was all attention. A working day stretched out ahead of him.

He bought a paper at the kiosk. He preferred French to Russian and right wing to left. On the bus there was a pretty girl, and he looked at her for a long time. He was curious about women and liked to observe ones he didn't know: how they powdered themselves, what they talked about, how they fixed their hair, how they crossed their legs.

He got off at a broad, deserted street where at that hour only the dogs were out and the maids walking the dogs chatted to each other. A dark blue-grey poodle covered with curls except for a shaved back stepped out of his way.

He walked past gardens. The wind rustled among the fallen leaves. Damn it, what a garden, what a house! White house, black door – and you don't hear a thing because you're stepping across something sandlike, so thick and deep it's like leaving tracks in velvety dust.

One tall mirror was reflected in another, and there, in that other one, he saw the edge of a laden table, a wisp of steam over a cup, and someone's elbow, and another door, and you couldn't tell which way to go: through that one, through the mirror, or through that closer one, where the hand of an elderly clean-shaven man wearing a butler's coat and a pince-nez on a black cord was beckoning to him.

'Tell him Mr Astashev is here,' said Alexei Georgievich without changing the expression on his ruddy face. He had a name, and he never attempted to explain in the foyer what it meant, why he had come.

The study was white, like a hospital ward,

with white leather furniture so deep that the couch and armchair were just waiting to swallow up anyone who sat in them. Into the white of the rug, the armchair, the telephone and the glass desk, and through the white door walked a big, powerfully built man with an expression of absolute boredom on his face. He looked at Alexei Georgievich, shook his head, and leaned his two fists on the desk, preparing to listen.

'I'll only keep you five minutes, not a second longer,' said Astashev ponderously, gravely, as if he wanted to impress him at the very outset with his youth and reliability. His blue eyes spoke with purity and lucidity of his integrity, his straightforwardness, his Orthodox christening, of the fact that had it gone a little further nature would have transformed them into the eyes of a young woman, a nun who had selflessly yielded to fate. 'Allow me to inform you of some important news.'

'How much is it going to cost me?' the businessman asked in a hoarse and careless voice, not yet aware of who it was before him. His heavy torso balanced on top of spread legs.

'Not a penny, if you decide not to take advantage of it. I came to tell you something that will seem like an awful truism to you:

We are all mortal. Fyodor Grigorievich sent me to you.'

'I don't know any Fyodor Grigorievich,' said the businessman, with an impenetrable look.

'Here is my watch: I promised not to keep you long. It tells me the time. One day it will tell *us* the time. Yes, yes, let us not shut our eyes to it: the bell will toll for each and every one of us.'

The businessman dropped his fists, nudged the armchair with his foot, and sank into it.

'What do you want from me?'

'I came here to remind you' – and Alexei Georgievich also lowered himself, but with caution, so as not to drown. 'We all persist in unforgivable thoughtlessness. After all, sooner or later *it* will come for you. Then I'm going to come and see your wife, then your children. I'm going to come and take a look at you. Have you thought about that?'

He rested his chin on his half-empty, soft briefcase and looked dreamily into the distance.

'We are giving you the opportunity to provide for your family – there'll be nothing to worry about. You'll have plenty to think over at the last moment as it is – your soul, for instance. I'm not a believer myself, but many are. In any event, it is frightening, and it happens to everyone no matter what. We are giving your nearest and dearest the opportunity to abandon themselves one hundred percent to their grief without having to worry about their daily bread during those first few days. Oh, those first few days! We pay reliably, promptly, gladly. We pay faster than the Banque de France, while you're laid out, while the deceased is still laid out on the table. You can make direct payment to insure yourself in the event of death, which will come one way or another.'

'Ah, so that's who you are.' The businessman stretched out his well-manicured white hand and wiped it across his dark tough face.

Alexei Georgievich went on, a little more calmly now.

'You'll pay every first of the month. I advise you to insure yourself for a million. The usual amount. Every man has moments when he thinks about his own end. Forgive me for speaking so candidly, so frankly about it, but we are alone after all. Those moments are terrible because whatever it is that awaits us is inescapable. Do you understand? Inescapable. As inescapable as the fact that today, whatever the weather, night will come. You can make phone calls, buy, sell, rush about, or go to sleep right now on this sofa. It makes no difference. Night will still come. And *it* will come too. That's it.' Astashev pinched the tender white flesh on his hand. 'All this will come to an end. And then what?'

A pause — two seconds. Then the blue poodle he'd seen in the street pushed the door open with its solid frame and walked in, leapt slowly and confidently onto the sofa, walking across and leaving tracks on the morocco leather, the rug, the morocco pillow. The businessman neither saw it nor stirred.

'What a marvellous animal. May I ask your age?'

'What's it to you? And anyway, why . . .?'

'You mean you can't guess? The closer to the end, the larger the payments: the greater the odds. At fifty there are certain odds and at sixty others. At seventy . . . But you're not seventy. You can't fool me! Just your signature will take care of everything.'

'Greater chances of what?' He was slowly turning pale, as if he were growing tired right then and there and didn't have the strength to chase away, to cut off this visitor.

'Of turning into a heavy, burdensome, and rapidly decaying object. You're probably sitting there thinking, why should I take out insurance when I have property, capital, bonds . . .? Let me tell you a story, a true story. I went to see a very important scholar – I won't say "great" because I never call anyone that on principle. The scholar said, "Forgive me, but why should I take out insurance? I have ten volumes of scholarly work, each one a thousand pages long. That's enough for my children and grandchildren as well." What do you think happened? Less than two years passed, he died, and some young upstart came along with a pamphlet he had thrown together exposing the old man, and now those ten volumes' – Alyosha suddenly gave a sharp whistle – 'and the widow is going hungry, actually going hungry.'

The businessman sat up with a start, looked at the dog's pawprints, and imperceptibly let out a slow deep breath.

'Thank you. I'll think it over,' he said. And he did indeed make it seem as if he were planning to give serious thought to what he had just heard. 'Good day.'

'Just one more thing,' Astashev exclaimed, as the businessman was already preparing to scramble out of the armchair on his sturdy legs. 'Of all things, do not think, or think about it as little as possible. Your signature is all.' He shook a piece of light-blue patterned cardboard out of his briefcase. 'Right here in the corner. I remember a singer (a famous baritone, I can't tell you his name – professional confidence) who thought and thought and then he died. Can we ever know what's going to happen to us?'

'Go. Enough,' said the businessman staring straight ahead. The yellowed whites of his swollen eyes looked like a child's cheap plastic toy. 'You've left your mark, Teacher, so get out. Out! General, take Teacher out.'

The butler with the pince-nez on the cord came in and took the poodle out. The businessman stirred heavily and started to climb out of his chair. Alexei Georgievich shot out of his like a coiled spring.

'Be sensible,' he said, again clearly, honestly, and loyally. 'If we don't know what's going to happen to us *there*, at least we can put our affairs in good order *here*.'

'Leave me,' pronounced the businessman very quietly, as if he were addressing some third party standing between them and Astashev, or even the armchair that wouldn't let him go.

Finally he got up. The deadly boredom on his face had become even gloomier, and there was something frightening about the cast of his expression.

'I'll leave you my card,' said Astashev.

Once again his pink fingers went into action, scooping up something that had slipped out of his briefcase.

'No need. I'm very busy. General, show the insurance agent out.'

Alexei Georgievich roused himself and walked to the door, and other doors, lacquered doors, glass doors. He was all attention. He already had a new address in his head. The trees stormed in the gardens he was passing. He was swinging his umbrella. There were no more dogs, or maids either for that matter. Chauffeurs were standing at attention by their automobiles waiting for their employers, and two Chinese cooks were walking to market, debating something in their ringing language.

Passing. Passing pleasant, tantalising thoughts of what the cooks would bring back from market: lobster, partridges, pineapple. He thought: Does the businessman have a wife? Probably a silly, capricious woman who loses at the casino in summer and eats too many pastries with whipped cream. Does the businessman have a daughter? Doubtless an easily bored, amorous creature with her sights set on a foreigner (the right approach!). How could he find them? Or talk to them? Maybe he has a son? Yes, of course, he does have a son, and his address is even entered in Astashev's little book. A film production business, a starstudded office twinkling away under that very sky, on the Champs-Élysées. Go there tomorrow, cajole him, apply some pressure, reel in some contacts, and leave a mark there as well. But that was for tomorrow. He had three more appointments for today.

The city, the streets, this race to meet life head on. He swam along in it freely and easily, he was comfortable in it – citizen, taxpayer . . . but not a soldier! He had not changed his citizenship, naturally. 'A Frenchman in spirit,' he often said, but he carried the same useless international passport, which had in fact been no hindrance to him at all. He had no wish to link his fate, his warm, precious, secure, unique life with an entire country, with a state that was not always peaceful and that, at times, went through upheaval. He kept his money in an American bank in case times got rough. He could hop on a train, or a boat, or a plane and keep his happy, industrious, and yet vulnerable existence going at full tilt.

'From Ivan Stepanovich Besser,' he uttered with a bow as he entered the stale but spacious drawing room cluttered with cheap antiques, deriving a certain satisfaction from shaking the soft hand of its owner which felt as if it had just been washed. 'Excuse me if I'm interrupting, but Ivan Stepanovich urgently requested that I stop by to see you.'

'Sit down, sit down, dear man.' A short, tubby, rusty-haired man, with large intelligent eyes, led him to a small table where flowers trembled precariously in a vase.

'I'll take up a minimum of your time and will inform you – alas! – what I am obliged by my profession to say: sooner or later the curtain will fall.'

His host gasped and wrung his hands.

'Oh, I know what you mean. Don't remind me. It's dreadful! Haven't they invented something for that yet? You know there was an article in America about some kind of pill . . . And they call this progress!'

Alexei Georgievich smiled.

'What pills? Come now, everything on earth, from the tiniest insect to the greatest genius, has its end. Can pills really do anything about that?'

'Then they should say what's *there*! What use are all their academies and universities and laboratories? No, no, I refuse to talk about that. I don't want to. Let's change the subject. I know, Ivan Stepanovich insured himself for a hundred thousand. I've decided to insure myself for a hundred thousand, too. I'm even going to insure my wife for a hundred thousand (will you give me a discount for two?). But we're going to handle the whole thing discreetly. We're not going to think about the meaning of what we're doing. I'm not going to be able to sleep tonight. I'm too scared.'

Astashev smiled once more and nodded slightly in assent.

'Then let's not. I've already forgotten what we were talking about. If struggle is impossible we must take measures to see that it all goes smoothly, as discreetly as possible, that the payment is made – '

'Ah, by the way, I'm told you're not always prompt about paying.'

'Prompter than the Bank of England.'

'But you sometimes get taken to court?'

'Just by cranks. I beg you not to say such a thing, even in jest.'

'Ah, how interesting. You mean there are cranks? And do you pay for suicides?'

'What on earth for?' Astashev made an ugly face. 'With one foolhardy act a man cancels out his entire life. Why reward him? That just makes him someone who never existed, a chimera. We pay for a normal end.

And therefore we can only pay for people who were, who existed, not suicides.'

'Most interesting. Go on, please. I'll get my wife.'

He stood up, opened the door to the adjoining room, and said lovingly:

'Darling, come on in . . . That's all right. Our guest doesn't mind.'

A woman came in. Her hair was uncombed and she wore a housecoat. She had a broad Russian face and a full ungirdled figure.

'I beg of you, go on.'

Alexei Georgievich, taking up the woman's point of view, quickly sketched out the business that had brought him.

'Well, that's clear,' said the hostess, combing her fingers through her hair. 'Everyone in America took out insurance a long time ago. We're the ones who are behind the times.'

Documents with seals, documents with writing, documents with blanks that needed filling in slipped out of the briefcase and into Astashev's hands. He quickly located the right amount on the chart and made some calculations.

'Isn't that interesting, darling,' said the host, signing first here, then there. 'One of us will collect on the other.'

'Well, naturally. It works out very nicely.'

Alexei Georgievich blotted the signatures first here, then there, with a square of pink blotting paper.

'When does it come into effect?'

'This very minute.'

'Do you hear that, darling? Isn't that interesting. We're already insured.'

She signed where she had to as well, and they immediately wrote Astashev a cheque, despite his protests. He put everything back in his briefcase, clipped his pen to his pocket, and started saying goodbye. They thanked him for what seemed like forever, tried to talk him into staying for lunch, and gave him the address of a family acquaintance ('Zhenya Sokolova's uncle. You probably know him.') who had wanted to for a long time . . .

When they reached the door Astashev asked when he could send the doctor by.

'Oh, don't bother, don't bother,' exclaimed the host with tears in his voice. 'He'll just find all sorts of diseases. That's right, darling, isn't it? He shouldn't bother.'

But Astashev said he couldn't go ahead without it, so they agreed. Then they thanked him again and asked him to thank Ivan Stepanovich for his unfailing concern for them.

It was lunchtime. Every day he had lunch in a clean, inexpensive, rather institutional-looking restaurant where they knew him well and where the same people always sat on his right, people from the south who ate an extraordinary amount of very good food, and a thin woman with a big nose and a brightly painted mouth sat on his left. He made no exceptions, even on Sundays. He ate slowly, read the newspaper, did some calculations in its margins, made notes in his little book, worked things out in his head, occasionally asked to see the directory and carefully turned its pages between the plates. He never drank wine; he was served a bottle of mineral water. A few words about the weather to the garçon, a nod in the direction of the big-nosed woman (hadn't she grown prettier since yesterday?), a half-bow to his neighbours. Poached fish and roast meat, or roast meat and dessert, coffee, cake. Three lumps of sugar in a small white cup with a crack. After lunch he went to wash his hands, clean his nails, tidy his hair with the comb and thick brush he carried with him, and brush the dandruff and crumbs off his shoulders. Then he left – with his umbrella and briefcase in his hands and a new route, a new address, in his head. He moved along this urban conveyor belt that knew no beginning, no end, and no pause. He was conveyed, moved along, like a spoke or a screw, and to do so came to him as naturally as it does to a tree to grow in the same place.

'*Permettez.*'

But they wouldn't let him in. The door opened a crack, an eye glittered, and a man's voice said:

'Yes, it's me. Who are you?'

'I already came once, but I missed you. I – '

'Are you selling brushes? Sewing machines?'

Alexei Georgievich tried to edge in with one shoulder.

'I make the hardest thing of all a little easier. I sell life insurance.'

The door gave way but immediately closed shut on him, catching him so that the umbrella was inside but the briefcase was stuck on the outside.

'Go away!' And the person standing in the foyer jangled something metal in his hand. It was a set of keys. 'Are you insuring *against* life?'

'What do you mean, against life?' That caught Astashev off his guard. And the thought flashed briefly: Could something like that really be done?

'Go to hell!' shouted the man, squeezing him in the door harder and harder. 'I'd rather be shot of it. You can't frighten me! What I want is someone to insure me against life, this bloody life.'

'If you don't mind, I don't deserve . . . I have something very important to tell you.'

'That no one lives forever? Well, all the better. That's just what I'm waiting for.'

'But your wife, your children,' prattled Alexei Georgievich as he tried to free himself from the crack. 'To leave them unprovided for – '

'Wife? Children?' the voice exclaimed hysterically. 'Leave money to that old idiot for her lover? To those little bastards to bet on the horses? Get out. You're not needed here.'

'No one has ever spoken to me like – '

'Out! Out!' And Astashev felt something pressing on his chest and shoving him. He summoned all his strength and darted sideways out of the door. It slammed in his pink face so hard that it shook the house. 'They've been hanging around here since the morning,' moaned the voice behind the door. 'Vacuums! Typewriters!'

Astashev spat coarsely, landing just above the keyhole. 'Barbarians,' he said loudly. 'Mongols.' He descended the steps slowly, opened his umbrella because it was drizzling, and walked off, calming himself, letting his blood cool. And suddenly he remembered he still had one more place to go, one more name. A rendezvous set for today. The most intriguing thing he had to do.

But before making that rendezvous – a visit to the sculptor Engel, whom he had already been to see twice without managing to come to terms with him on either occasion – he decided to stop off at the insurance company he represented. He usually passed by most days, usually in the late afternoon.

Nearly two hundred employees and at least a hundred clients crowded into a big hall that was divided up by grilles. In the grilles were small openings, and above each opening there was a number and a sign. Astashev shook several hands, slapped someone lightly on the back, and having received a gentle slap on the shoulder in return, went over to window 53, above which was written 'Deaths'. Now that his French was perfect, though, he knew that the word 'death' never crossed the lips of the moustached, middle-aged, high-collared employee who sat at that window. What he heard was the word 'decease', which sounded so much more agreeable to the client's ear.

He took care of everything for the two policies signed that day, set up a doctor's visit, obtained the necessary blanks (supplementary to the blue patterned papers), and graciously acknowledged the comments about how he was one of the most successful agents in the company's entire hundred-year existence. Only then did he find out that the day before they had got word of the death of a client whom he had insured eight years ago. He promised to stop by to pay a call tomorrow, told the young lady sitting at the back of the 'Deaths' section to find the file for that case, and while she was taking one of the first policies marked by his hand out of a thick file, turned to chat at the next window, under the sign 'Personal Accidents'.

At five o'clock he was already at Engel's.

Blocks of clay wound in wet rags, a piece of stone torso with spread legs, the square beaten-up face of a famous boxer just cast in bronze with the crown of the head lopped off and an overgrown bronze cauliflower ear were stacked up in the chilly, high-ceilinged studio where he was ushered in by Engel himself, a dry, small man with no beard and no eyebrows, who looked Japanese and wore a long white smock.

'I've been expecting you. Eagerly,' he said, spreading his thin greenish lips to show a mouth full of heavy, close-set teeth that made his whole weak, fragile face jut forward. 'You did such an astounding job last time explaining about why you'd come. I've been hoping I'd get to listen to you some more. It was so odd, what you were saying. As if you'd been sent from the next world as a reminder. (You don't talk with everyone like that, now, do you?) But I couldn't then. I had a model sitting here, there, that one (he poked a childish hand at a stone torso, and it seemed incredible that such a giant had visited him and not crushed him). I've thought a lot about all that since then. It was the first time I'd ever had to think about it. And I realised that my conviction that there isn't anything *there* makes living impossible. Do you smoke?'

'I don't smoke and I don't philosophise,' said Astashev, moving from the shaky stool he had sat down on for some reason to the soft upholstered sofa in the corner of the studio. 'Last time you and I were talking about two hundred thousand. Given your relative youth, it's really worth it.'

'Fine,' Engel replied, wiping his low sallow forehead pensively and deliberately with two fingers. 'But that's not the most important thing. You came to see me with your talk about the fifth act, the final curtain, the finale, saying that everything has an end. All those metaphors which were hardly in the best taste. That's what's important – terribly important for me. You've become indispensable to me. I thought you might make it possible for me to think this whole horror show through to the end.'

'I'm flattered.'

'There's something offensive about you . . . But we can talk about you later. First let's talk about me, because I haven't slept for ages, and I haven't been able to work at all for almost two weeks now. I've started to doubt everything. I've started to think that if there's a *here* then there has to be a *there*. That is, it's impossible that there's nothing *there* if there's something *here*. I've lost some of my conviction, and that's made things a little easier for me.'

'If you please,' exclaimed Astashev, and he smiled the most simple-hearted of his smiles, 'what kind of *there* can there be? You're not sixteen anymore. You're experienced, you've lived. You're probably even – don't be offended – a bit of a libertine. What kind of doubts can there be that there isn't anything *there* at all? What have you come across *here* that could have made you so wrong about *there*? Good food, young women, the beauty of nature, comfort, security?'

'No, there's got to be more to it,' said Engel adamantly, and he looked closely at Astashev.

'God help me then, because I don't see it. And believe me, when I say "good food" I'm talking about the rarest of delicacies, not about stuffing yourself stupid every day. And as for women: there was a time when people blushed, perspired, sighed (perhaps not me personally), but by now everyone realises perfectly well what love consists of. Even the women. And if they don't—so much the worse for them.'

'No, that's not it at all. I don't know myself, but there's more to it than that. There's no other way.'

'Art? Literature? There used to be that. People read until daybreak, got swept up in politics (though I never have). But by now they know better. They've learned. What's left?'

Engel walked away to the window and looked out at the September twilight.

'But if you think that, then how can you live? How can you die?'

'How can you live? Listen to this: I was on my way to see a client today. A male dog was having it off with a bitch on the pavement.

And do you know what I said to myself? How simple happiness is!' He laughed.

Engel went back to the sofa, stubbed his cigarette out in a saucer, and said slowly:

'But what's someone supposed to do who can't be like that?'

'Try to make things as logical as possible. Watch his health, work, live like everyone else does. Take out insurance. The state rests on people like you and me, not on dreamers and failures. It is the collective guarantee of sober people to facilitate their own life and death.'

'No, that won't do.'

Astashev peeked at his watch under his cuff, fumbled with the booklet in his hands, and then put it back down beside him.

'My objective is modest,' he said, as if excusing himself. 'To remind people that the inevitable will come and that they should prepare for it well in advance and in the most advantageous and convenient way possible.'

Engel's slanted eyes fixed once more with a kind of melancholy hope on Alexei Georgievich's smooth round face. Neither said anything.

'I can imagine,' Engel now spoke more dispassionately, 'the kind of experiences you've had with people. I bet your presence makes a lot of them very uneasy. Perhaps you should write your memoirs? But maybe you're writing them now?'

Astashev drew himself up.

'I place very high demands on literature,' he said with dignity. 'If I were a writer I would delve deep into the human spirit and write somewhere between Tolstoy and Dostoevsky, but in French.'

Again neither said anything. Finally Astashev, who had been casting around in his thoughts for the broken thread, found the words he'd been looking for:

'And so, allow me to draw the bottom line. You're frightened, you're confused. But you can't stop thinking about the practical aspect of the matter. Today I've brought along all the necessary papers. Since you're under forty it can all be taken care of without a medical examination. We just need one test, and if there's no sugar – '

'Listen,' said Engel with childlike amazement. 'Why should I insure myself? I'm completely alone. I don't have a wife, or children, or nephews. I live, work, and sell. I give money to whoever needs it and asks me for it. A suit lasts me for four years and I eat nothing but vegetables. I'm not going to take out insurance.'

Astashev stood up sharply.

'Excuse me,' he said loudly and bad-temperedly. 'This is the third time I've come to see you and sat here and explained. My time is valuable. Why do you keep inviting me here? If you haven't got anyone to insure yourself for, you should have told me that before. You're committing a grave error: you're young, you're healthy, you could insure yourself for your retirement.'

'Don't get angry, please,' said Engel. He turned his back to Astashev. 'I asked you to come because it seemed to me you knew something. You probably don't notice yourself what it is you're dodging. Just tell me one thing: How do you think it will come?'

Astashev was already putting on his coat in the entryway.

'It will come as it does for a hare in a hunt or a fly in a glass,' he said angrily. 'I'm a self-made man, and those trivialities don't concern me.'

He picked up his umbrella and briefcase, raised his hat, and without saying another word, left. Engel wiped his perspiring palms with a handkerchief and went to the window to watch him go. The window of the studio looked out on the square and he saw Astashev emerge, walk away, hail a taxi, get in it, and drive away.

The day was drawing to a close. As usual the lift wasn't working at Klavdia Ivanovna's. He drank tea and she knitted. Today they talked politics, and Alyosha tried to explain to his mother that the proletariat were the people who smelled. Then he left, and by the time he got to Xenia Andreevna's he was completely unwound and happy.

'Mamenka,' he said, taking a bite of cold veal and choosing a moment when the admiral and governor weren't listening, 'yesterday I went from here to the Tabarain . . . with two can-can dancers. We were out very late, and I gave them caviar and champagne. Give me the address of Doctor Markelov just in case. We parted on good terms.'

She nodded her head with unconcealed satisfaction and replied in her low whisper:

'Sit back a little, gravedigger. I can smell the corpses on you.'

III

He had met her two years before. She was

living with her two old aunts in the same building as Xenia Andreevna, but downstairs, and once she stopped in to say that if Vyazminitinov came he should come down because someone had been to see them that day who had seen his son recently in Moscow. In short, she had come to deliver a message. Mamenka didn't even look at her: Fine, I'll tell him. But when Vyazminitinov came she forgot all about Zhenya, and the next day Zhenya had to come again. She begged her pardon for the inconvenience and left Vyazminitinov a note. Astashev was there again. He got up, said hello, asked whether Zhenya had been to see the popular play that featured the actress with the magnificent bosom. Zhenya blushed. Her eyes glittered, and she said she didn't go to theatres at all because she was busy every evening.

'And the cinema?' he asked, appraising her more attentively.

'Oh, every day,' she replied. 'I sell the tickets.'

She was wearing a dark blue woollen dress with buttons that ran down her flat chest from collar to waist.

'What exceedingly original buttons,' said Astashev. He wanted to touch one of them. She recoiled, and her eyes darkened (they were light brown). Quickly gathering up her fair, gold-flecked hair and coiling it at her nape, she turned to go. And suddenly he noticed that she was slim and graceful, on the tall side, with a high waist and long straight legs.

'Her mother has remarried. To Count Loder,' said Xenia Andreevna. 'Her aunts are halfwits who keep her under lock and key. And she's innocent. I'd lay odds on it. A virgin. It's phenomenal, but it's a fact.'

A week later he ran into her at the main entrance.

He was on his way out, and she was coming in from work.

'Right here.' He pointed to her black purse. 'This is where you carry the cash box.'

'No,' she replied, 'I turn the money over to the owner. He comes by for it.'

'Oh well, too bad. Otherwise I could have robbed you in some alley.'

She smiled, confused.

'For some reason there's a gun at the ticket office,' she said trustingly. 'I haven't the faintest idea why it's there though. I don't know how to shoot.'

'Are there really ever such large amounts of money there?'

'That's just it. There aren't. I think someone just forgot it, or dropped it. I've had five gloves lying there for, oh, a year – all for the right hand. Also two sets of keys, a compact, a lighter, and a stickpin with a fake stone. They're just there.'

'Would you like to take a little walk? It's early still, and it's a fine evening.'

'No,' she said. 'They're expecting me at home.'

And as if she hadn't quite finished saying something, she gave him her thin hand in its suede glove.

'You never flirt, and you always go home on time?'

'I never flirt and never have,' she replied, and left.

'But she's gorgeous, just gorgeous! Sweet, innocent, delicate, young. She has such a happy look and sad voice. Odd she hasn't married before. She's probably almost thirty,' he thought en route. But by the next day he was no longer thinking of her, and when he ran into her again on the stairs a month later he didn't recognise her.

He turned around, and she turned around at the same time, and in the darkness both of them stopped.

'You're back from work? So late?'

'Always at the same time, a quarter to eleven.'

'And tomorrow, too? Every day?'

She suddenly collected herself and didn't answer, sneaking a look but not looking.

'You're prettier than when I saw you last,' he said. 'How are the buttons doing? Still there? And still no flirting?'

She slowly opened her long rouged lips, showing her white, even, narrow teeth, and said gravely:

'Not counting you.'

And she left the darkness of the lower landing. When he switched on the light her steps died and a door slammed shut somewhere.

Every evening he met her, but on the street, not on the stairs. They talked for a few minutes, and they always found something to talk about. He walked with her to her building, listening to her stories about work, about her aunts, about her mother, about her girl-friends.

'Are they pretty?' he asked.

And she answered, 'Not very. Like me.'

'From the fact that you come to see Xenia Andreevna every evening I've come to the conclusion that you don't have anyone to flirt with now either,' she once said, smiling with embarrassment. 'Not counting me.'

But he answered with unexpected frankness.

'No flirting, but there is a lady I know. She has a corset shop. She's French, of course. One can go and see her as late as twelve at night. Before that there's not much to do there. But I have a feeling she's going to start boring me pretty soon. You don't know men. We're awful swine. Of course, that's just what women love us for.'

She walked to the door with a firm tread and, saying goodbye, pale, announced that her holiday began the next day.

'What, in the middle of winter? Where are you going to go?'

'Nowhere. Is it really absolutely obligatory to go somewhere?'

Then her aunts moved to another apartment. He never asked after Zhenya, but sometimes he remembered her as a very frail, slender, flexible plant, almost translucent, and a little poisonous. Then he forgot about her.

The aunt who had the money died, and Zhenya and the other aunt could not touch the inheritance. Months passed, and life got hard. It was being challenged, the trial date was approaching, but the will was never found. Life changed completely – restricted now in every aspect and very quiet. Zhenya had worked all her life; she had always supported herself. But now there were two living on her salary. Moreover, the aunt who was alive was weak and constantly ill, and there was no one to turn to for help because she was the sister of Zhenya's father, and Zhenya's mother had not been on speaking terms with her for a long time.

Day and night Zhenya sat in the ticket window of the small, elegant cinema, so that the customers only saw her hands, her delicate fingers and their long, dark-red, lacquered nails, and the agate ring set in platinum. Sometimes someone buying a ticket tried to bend over, breathe into the opening in the glass, and take a look at her face, but she just jotted something down in pencil without raising her head, tore off a green ticket, and handed out silver and copper change from the cash box. Her hands kept taking in those ticket booklets, dozens of them, which she carefully hid in the box, the same box that held the five lost gloves, compact, and lighter. And every so often the hope crept up on her, as furtively as a cat, that Astashev would all of a sudden show up – not for her, not to see her, but at the cinema, as a viewer. That he would buy a ticket from her and she would shake his hand through the low-cut glass.

She was living far away now, on the opposite bank of the Seine, and no longer had any chance of running into him at night. She thought of those past encounters when — or so it seemed to her — he had been waiting for her, with something like madness. She thought about how here she'd been living her life for such a long time and she knew nothing about him. Did he still go to see Xenia Andreevna? Was he still seeing the corset shop owner? Did he still smile broadly and gaily, did he still dress fastidiously, was he still a little overweight as before?

She felt such sadness some mornings when, sleepy, still in her dressing-gown, blue smudged under her eyes, she stood over the bubbling percolator and thought about writing him a letter. In fact, she had already composed the first sentence:

'Evgenia, you should call me Evgenia, dear Alexei Georgievich, because I am writing you this letter, exactly like Tatiana in the opera . . .'

On those mornings she realised she would never write to him, never seek his affection, or his name.

'But what shall I do? What can I do?' she asked her large, drab window, which let the cold in during the winter and in the summer a warm rustle of fragrant bushes from the neighbour's garden far below, as if it were the bottom of a well.

Days were either dreamy and melancholy or else so busily tedious that his voice, his manner, his whole being flickered in her memory, and when she was finally left to herself, weary, it reappeared and seemed fainter and somehow more touching.

She did not have her own room. She slept in the dining room, and her aunt slept in the next. That was now the sum total of their living quarters. Zhenya never went visiting and never invited anyone as she was too busy for chitchat and anyway was incapable of making conversation. Gradually she even stopped seeing her mother because she felt as if she were an embarrassment to her – and little by little she drew apart from her girl-friends as well. There was no doubt about it: she was poor, and she was lonely. She had been condemned by fate to a lacklustre life bereft of happiness, bereft of rapture, so that her innate elegance, her long eyes, her sleek, smooth, golden hair, and her long legs, which she liked to put into rough shoes and thin stockings so that the hairs poked through and the birthmark on her ankle was clearly visible, seemed almost incongruous.

The obese old lady got around with great difficulty. Insulted by the litigation over the inheritance and accustomed to an idle and well-provided life, she sometimes did not say a word for days on end. Zhenya wrote the letters to the lawyers for her, fed her her meals in bed or in her easy chair, and then left for work. She watched before her the changing line of people come to be entertained as if in a dream. Thus her day passed, and she thought about how that was life and how sometimes there was misery on top of that as well.

Almost without having thought about it — later, she couldn't work out how it had happened — one day, in the autumn, after nearly a year and a half had passed since she had seen Astashev, she had the idea of paying Xenia Andreevna a call. They found someone to fill in for her at the cinema that night, and she went out wearing the same dark blue woollen dress — not knowing herself what she intended to accomplish and unable to explain this action to herself — and returned to the street where she had once lived.

The building seemed utterly foreign and gloomy to her. The entrance stirred up memories. But nothing had really happened. He hadn't told her anything definite, and she didn't care what he said anyway. But she still couldn't manage to come up with an excuse to explain why she had come.

But an excuse turned out to be utterly unnecessary. Xenia Andreevna was in an excited, keyed-up state, and she included Zhenya in her powerful, suffocating embraces. Besides Astashev there were two other guests, neither of whom Zhenya knew.

'Zhenechka Sokolova,' said Astashev. 'Can I offer you a liqueur with mustard?'

And suddenly he felt an animal joy from her presence.

She drank in tiny sips and smiled. And she was amazed at the air, which made you breathe in a completely different way from anywhere else on earth. There was something heady about this silk-draped, still straight-backed, painted, older woman and in the two men, who were obviously infected by this headiness and who were courting her in a crude and passionate way. And finally there was something special about Astashev, Alyosha Astashev, as she called him to herself, something suddenly strange, near and momentous that changed her forever.

'Well, if you'd really like to, then that's that. Go ahead,' he said, forgetting that he himself had only just now asked her to tell how she had been occupying herself all that time. But she was silent, her pale face shining as she looked into his round blue eyes.

'You have such blue eyes. Only children and very old men have eyes like that,' she said with great love.

'I've been told that a million times.' He flashed his teeth, and she noticed a new gold tooth on one side of his mouth. 'Listen, my sweetheart, have you ever kissed a man?'

'No,' she replied, and shook her golden hair.

'What a little fool you must be then!'

They both laughed. And suddenly she felt like confessing. She sat for another five minutes without moving or speaking while he told her an 'absolutely true story' from his own life, and although it had something to do with a woman, Zhenya was too preoccupied with what was going on inside her to make sense of what he was telling her.

'I don't know him at all. Why should I love him? For his beauty? But he probably doesn't seem wonderful to anybody but me, and can I really love somebody just for being handsome? Look how coarsely he eats, and anyway, if he were really that handsome he would have been married a long time ago. There's no such thing as a handsome bachelor. Maybe I love him because of the attention he pays me? But where's the attention? Once he asked me about the buttons on this dress, but that doesn't prove he was thinking about me. I love him for all of it, for his crudeness, for his obvious meanness, for his bandit's laugh, for the boorish way he moves.'

'I must confess, Zhenechka, I've never kissed anyone either.' He made a guilty face. 'There was never time. Other things – well, I'm not saying, but as for kisses – I just never had time. Generally speaking I've always been in a dreadful rush. And, you know, when I was sixteen there was an alarm clock in the cook's room that made a terrible noise, a real din. Why, I never even took the time to find out whether it was on a chest of drawers, or a windowsill, or even on a shelf of some kind. Good Lord! Life is too short, and there's too much to do.'

'What if this was the limit of possible happiness,' the thought occurred to her, 'and there could never be better moments than this, ever?'

'You know what would be the most interesting thing right now?' said Alexei Georgievich. 'Let's go somewhere. We might even go to your cinema. We can take the best seats in the house.'

'No. Why go to the cinema? It's too late anyway. And today the film isn't particularly good.'

'Well then, let's go to the Fair. I still haven't been to the Fair. Have you?'

'I went with my aunt, but I hardly saw anything.'

'With your aunt. Well, today you can go with your uncle. Only you won't see anything this time either.'

It was the autumn, and the year of the World's Fair, the one that disfigured Paris for a few months and then vanished into thin air leaving no mark or monument behind it, nothing except the memory of a chaotic profusion of lights, objects and crowds.

When they walked onto the bridge they were in the middle of a dense crowd that pressed in on all sides (Astashev led Zhenya by the arm to make sure he didn't lose her), and overhead, in the moonlit September sky, a prolonged salvo of fireworks was blazing away. It was already night, and this gaiety, which amazed rather than infected the visitors, was already on the wane. Under the bridge, in the sluggish Seine made violet by the reflected fountains, lights trembled, flickered, flared, and danced. Rockets shot straight up from its banks and exploded, and children's balloons fell to earth through the deep black heights. Thousands of balloons flowed across the sky like the Milky Way and were lost, the last of them resembling in colour and size the moon which sailed close by. From the Eiffel Tower wailed metallic music, a chorus of voices, and an organ whose grindings brought tears to the eyes. A siren screamed in the distance, and once again the gold of Roman candles spilled into the sky, falling into the blackness of a straying sailing cloud.

Everything was rocking – the water under the bridge, the crowd on the shore, the air shot with light. A lost child pressed to the rails of the bridge was crying. A policeman was trying to make his way to him through the density of swaying bodies. And breathing in the rocket smoke and that wailing music, it seemed to Zhenya that all this, this madness of a holiday, had been hurled down onto this city, into this evening, turning it into a place where there was no sorrow or sighs, no human wickedness, no deceit, no separations, no shabby dance-hall decorations. But all Zhenya could really hear was the chorus of her own heart, like a motorboat tearing across a lake of happy tears.

They sat on the bridge of a yacht until

everything was over. He told her that she should go home with him, that generally Russian women were dreadful teasers. Whenever a woman walked by he started following her with his eyes and made a comment.

'I have very specific tastes,' he said, sucking through a straw, his hat pushed to the back of his head. 'I like brunettes more than blondes. About five years ago I had this blonde. My God, how she messed me about. We men are awful swine. You've got a lot to learn, Zhenechka. I suggest you start taking instruction from me.'

Now it was no longer an impression. She knew for certain, clearly, that there would never be another evening like this. It was going to be the only one. And she had to do something to make it last, because the night and the morning were going to rip everything apart, throw everything into confusion, wreck her life. She wasn't thinking about why she loved him any more. Everything, from his name to his Russianness, which no number of French expressions could overcome, charmed her, oppressed her. Why did she think she had to explain or vindicate herself to anyone? She had never sat like this with a man before at night on the bridge of a moored yacht (which could have set off on a round-the-world cruise of fairy-tale lands, but which wouldn't leave, a yacht with its lights out). It seemed to her that together he and she could live a life unafraid, like love-birds, or half a life, or at least a quarter of a life. She had never felt like spending so much as twenty-four hours with anyone before. She thought about how she could stand by and help him do something, unnoticed and brave. And maybe something that he couldn't have done alone and she couldn't have done alone they could do together.

In total darkness the crowd flocked to the exits. Both of them walked quickly, with the rest, to the Metro stop. She was going one way; he the other.

'Come and tuck me in for the night,' he said, holding her hand in his. 'No one will ever find out. Don't be provincial.'

She tore her hand away, ran down the stairs, stopped, and looked back, remembering that he hadn't told her where or when they would see each other again. But he was already gone, and a crowd of tired, crumpled, dusty, sweaty people was piling on top of her. They bore her to the train and down the street right up to her doorstep, and someone even came in with her and followed her upstairs — but went up another floor. Then, when she was alone on her sofa in the dining room, where it always smelled of meals, tears suddenly poured down on her hands. She didn't know what to do about them, how to catch them, how to stop them. It had been too cruel, this approach by an utter stranger, a person like a million others, whom she hadn't known before, whom something had marked out for her, who had cast a long shadow over her world. In this approach she sensed destiny, the threshold of life, and clutching her breasts in both hands, she whispered his name.

The rain was coming down in sheets, the wind was howling, the cold, wet, and tedium were truly autumn-like when, after what were for Zhenya four very long, hard days, he came to see her at the cinema. It was about half past ten. She was handing over the cash box to the owner, the last show was in progress, and Astashev, seeing the owner, said to her calmly, '*Bonsoir, chérie,*' and shook out his umbrella. She lost her voice from sheer happiness and shame, finished counting up the money and tickets, and as she tidied things away, and locked up, and switched off the overhead light, looked at him several times and smiled. He was examining the posters on the walls with his back to her.

When they came out a taxi was already waiting.

'Where are we going?' she asked. 'It's already so late.'

Without speaking, he pushed her forward, and when they got into the taxi, not looking her in the face, said quickly and drily:

'I'm not the kind of man who embraces in cars. Don't be afraid. In the first place, it's clumsy and uncomfortable. In the second . . . How are you feeling today?'

'Where are we going?' she asked again and saw a bottle of champagne sticking out of his pocket.

'Zhenechka, Zhenechka,' he said with annoyance. 'You ask an awful lot of questions.'

'All my life has been a pledge,' she said softly and dropped her face in her hand. 'That's from *Onegin*.'

'A fine opera,' he responded and harrumph-ed.

'Do you like music?' And her face lit up with such joy that even he was surprised.

'I do. But I don't get much chance to listen to it. Well, here we are. This is it.'

They got out. Because of the rain, she ran straight inside. He paid the fare, opened his coat and stuffed the change in a side pocket, and walked right up to her, put his arms around her, pressed her against the door, kissed her, grabbed her by the elbows, and without giving her a chance to catch her breath, silently holding her, dragged her over to the stairs.

'Let me go, dear Alexei Georgievich. Let me go,' she whispered. 'I have something to say to you. I'm frightened. I'll come some other time. I'm not going to make a scene. I'll be quiet. Let me go.'

He twisted her arms painfully behind her with surprising skill, and greedily kissed her lips twice, touching her breasts. She caught his hand, not so much to make him stop as to prevent herself from falling. And still holding on like that, she followed him into his apartment.

When she left it was already very late. In the darkness she felt for the knob and looked down. There, very close, was the lift – she was on the landing of the first floor. Then she walked down the stairs, opened the door to the street, and stood there for a while. The few street-lamps had been turned down, and there was no one either to her left or to her right.

She set out on foot. She passed no more

than a dozen people, two policemen, a few motor cars, and one high farmer's cart loaded with cauliflowers on its way to the Central Market. She walked for nearly an hour. As she was walking over the bridge she stopped. The Seine, bloated by the rain, looked as turgid as lard. Zhenya crossed herself and leaned out over the water. At that moment someone rode by on a bicycle, and the rider's shadow passed over her. She straightened up and walked on. When she got home she saw that it was four o'clock.

She took off her hat but kept her coat on and cautiously entered her aunt's room in her stockinged feet. The old lady's breathing was heavy and regular. In the darkness Zhenya walked over to the bedside table, opened the drawer, and rummaged around in it, but whatever she was looking for she didn't find. Taking the drawer with her, she went into the kitchen, turned on the light, and started searching again. She came up with various medications: strophanthus, aspirin, and finally, what she'd been looking for — the veronal. But there were only eight tablets left in the glass vial. Then with the help of two kitchen towels and the breadknife she sealed up the door, extinguished the light, and turned on the gas.

'God,' she thought as she sat in front of the burner and looked out unblinkingly through the curtainless window where the sky, red from the lights, seemingly filled with smoke, hung low over the earth. 'God, if You exist, make me afraid, make me come to my senses. If You exist and if my soul wants it, make it so that at least my body turns back, holds me back from sin. If You exist, help me at least to react, even if it's only as an animal reacts . . . '

But then, while she held her mouth to the hissing rubber tap, what Zhenya felt was not disgust: she felt an even more passionate desire for death. And in truth, her broken body and her consciousness began to call out for extinction and darkness. In fact her soul, far from separating itself from her body, embraced it even more firmly, helping it along, moving down through the ringing of bells and the explosion of rockets into the white, vanishing, melting Milky Way. For one single minute her body and soul found themselves united in a miraculous whole. With unwieldy force, life boxed Zhenya once more about the ears, and everything went out in an oblivion that held no visions.

IV

'Congratulate me,' said Alexei Georgievich. 'Today I closed – or nearly closed – a deal I've been chasing for three weeks.'

A moustached middle-aged man wearing a high collar bent over towards him, and there were more murmurings in the adjoining windows.

'Bring out the champagne,' someone said.

Astashev was already nodding to the right and left.

'Without fail. Today. Not only that' – he stopped short for a second – 'today I made contacts – '

'Gentlemen, he's going to be a director,' exclaimed someone sitting behind a desk under a lamp.

'But I have no desire whatsoever to be a director,' Astashev laughed happily. 'I'm utterly content with my fate.'

He turned on his heel and walked out

between the desks, treating everyone he passed to cigarettes, which he had bought for just this purpose. Feeling light and sure of foot, he set out to roam the streets, to look at ties in shop windows. It was cloudy and cold, but today he was so full of himself that he noticed neither the weather nor the women. In a small seventh-floor office on the Champs-Élysées, where the only furniture consisted of an empty desk, a chair for the owner, and a leather armchair for a visitor, he had finally met the businessman's son, a Russian, but one who no longer spoke Russian, and he had promised to slip a million-dollar policy under his father's nose for his signature at an opportune moment.

Astashev had immediately adopted the tone of a hardened conspirator, keeping quiet when the ochre-powdered secretary entered abruptly. And when a celebrated pilot had appeared without being announced – a large fellow dressed in a garish coat, a tough man who, shortly before, had signed a contract in that office for a role in a film, and whose presence so affected the little room that even the voices seemed to change in tone – Alexei got up to go.

'Shouldn't you take out some insurance as well?' the director asked. 'After all, you're probably going to take a nosedive before anyone else. It's strange you haven't broken your neck already.'

The pilot tossed two large light-coloured gloves on the desk.

'The company insures us,' he said, throwing a quick glance at Astashev.

'That doesn't make any difference,' he replied. 'This is neither the time nor the place, but allow me to submit that your company insures you officially, as one of a group, but you could also do the same thing in an individual capacity. It's always more enjoyable to act as an individual. In my opinion, it's even more enjoyable to enter paradise as a traveller at your own risk than as part of a group excursion.'

'Rubbish! You have to pay insane prices for this individualism of yours.'

'People who fly pay eleven percent more than those of us who just creep along the ground.'

The director burst out laughing.

'He's trying to reassure you. Listen, give him your address. He'll stop by and give you a little tête-à-tête explanation of what awaits you in the next world.'

'I never talk about the next world,' Astashev said cheerfully. 'This one's enough for me. We're living in the capital of the world, not the desert.'

The pilot took a calling card out of a wide, patent leather wallet, and while fumbling with some photographs, handed it to Astashev.

'Stop by ... sometime,' he said nonchalantly. 'I live quite far out, though, in the suburbs. You have to take the train.'

Alexei Georgievich thanked them both and bowed low as he did so.

He was so at ease and so happy, he felt so fresh, young, and confident, that when he sipped his chartreuse at the bar where he was treating eight or so employees from the insurance company, he became even more cheerful and charming. He had had a good, tasty lunch, and by about two he was feeling that he had had enough for one day. Now he would arrange some minor diversion for himself, relax, and recuperate his strength before going to the suburbs the next morning to see the pilot. He never put anything off until later. He was always hot on the trail of something new.

Three hours later he was at Xenia Andreevna's. He had spent those three hours at a certain house where he had been merely an observer, not a participant, and that had taken more than enough out of him for today. They knew him at that house, which was expensive and only open during the daytime. When he appeared the doorman asked whether he wished the left door or the right. Behind the left door there were women; behind the right, an armchair and a screen. He alternated. Today it was his turn for the screen.

Xenia Andreevna was never at home at this hour, however. The servant opened the door for him, and he walked into the living room, took off his shoes, put his feet up on the sofa, picked up the newspaper, and ordered a cup of tea with lemon for himself. It was the evening paper, which he read for lack of anything better to do, and strangely, whether due to the state of his digestion or from having sat for so long in that stuffy and perfectly silent darkness, there was nothing in it that caught his interest, and drowsiness hovered quite close to hand.

He read the paper every day, and always with the same feeling: OK then, let's see what they've done now. What are they all worked up about today? Any news that concerned Russia aroused ridicule in him. So, gentlemen, you're still around? Then when he came upon photographs in which one man wearing

a first-rate pair of army boots greeted thousands wearing the same boots, something
inside him shivered secretly and happily.
That was exactly how he imagined power
should be, and like that only: the personal
and ultimate source of knowledge and authority.

And then he dreamed, and his dreams – as
with many people who don't know how to
dream properly – were abstract and clumsy,
far removed from the reality in which he
lived. He dreamed of order – of a man who
could hold in his hands all of Europe, and
thus the whole world as well. And then he,
Astashev, would get himself a pair of those
smart shiny boots, which would stand as a
mark of distinction for people adhering to a
great discipline. He would prove indispensable to the world, much more indispensable
than now, because now everyone was equal:
healthy and sick, scramblers and losers alike.
But then there would be just Astashevs.
Astashevs, Astashevs, and more Astashevs.

His eyes ran over the page: a mining
engineer in a fit of dementia had slit his wife's
and two children's throats; the dog show had
opened; subterranean tremors had been felt
on Formosa; the rising cost of electricity; a
ministerial crisis in Belgium; the suicide of

one Mademoiselle du Pont: her neighbour's attention was drawn by the strong smell of gas, and when they broke down the door . . . In a note she asked them to forgive her for the inconvenience and wrote that she was dying out of unrequited love.

When he woke up it was already completely dark in the room. Xenia Andreevna had not yet returned. He put his shoes on and wrote on a scrap of paper:

'Mamenka, how about going out somewhere and having a good time? Put on your most ravishingly low-cut dress. I'll come by at eight.'

And since he had absolutely nothing to do, he went by Klavdia Ivanovna's, whom he hadn't seen in all this time.

Klavdia Ivanovna was lying in her bed. Her teeth ached, and she had a fever. The room hadn't been tidied, and there was nothing good for tea.

'You know, Mamma,' he said, sitting by the bed. 'I hate to see you ill. Really, we could have sat a while and had a nice cosy chat.' He felt that his good mood had actually begun to slip even before this, even before his nap on the sofa.

'Five days you haven't been here,' she said, warming her puffy cheek with her hand. 'Are you well? Who have you been with? Have you been eating properly?'

He was suddenly sad and didn't answer right away.

'Has it really been five days? Mamma, I don't even notice how the time flies. It makes me a little sad. My youth will just pass me by like that – if it hasn't already! Why on earth have I started feeling so terrible? I was in such a great mood before. It's you that's had this effect on me. When you're ill everything else seems wrong. You're not getting up, Mamma? Really, if you'd just drink some tea . . . '

She shook her head.

'It's because you're still single, Alyosha.'

He undid the two lower buttons of his waistcoat, rested his elbows on his knees, and propped his face on his hands.

'What, get married?' he asked with derision, but there was a serious note in his voice, and Klavdia Ivanovna's heart started beating faster under the covers. 'Marry some modest young thing in love up to her ears? A Russian girl, they'll tell me. Yes, of course, but pure, nevertheless, awash with virtue. Goes around in the same dress for two years. Has a job.'

'Alyoshenka,' Klavdia Ivanovna moaned softly, afraid of frightening him off.

'She and I could build ourselves a little nest. After all, now I can . . . thank God! If not now, then when? I deserve it. Mamma, you'll laugh, but we would have the most freckle-faced children – both of us so fair.' He raised his head, touched the lamp burning on the night stand, and rocked on his chair.

'All that just popped into my head – idle dreams! More for you than myself. We could all move in together, and I'd give up all my bachelor pleasures. What man doesn't have dreams from time to time? We could have a maid, a poker-faced old maid. She'd do everything for us, and none of us would ever have to lift a finger again, right?'

Klavdia Ivanovna raised herself on her thin elbow and let a tear fall on her pillow.

'Are you in love, Alyosha?'

He looked at her, and suddenly a harsh, dry shadow crossed his light eyes.

'Mamma, you can't stop living in your fantasies, can you?' he said, and stood up. 'What am I, a schoolboy? If I'm going to marry, then there should at least be a dowry so that you, and we, and all of us could live in style.'

He was especially put out just now that he had said anything to her about a life as a threesome. That would mean giving up

Xenia Andreevna for good, and that, of course, was out of the question.

He left very quickly, with a heavy heart, recalling the note he had left for Xenia Andreevna and picturing where he might take her. There, in the living room, which was draped with silk scarves and pieces of oriental fabric, sat Vyazminitinov and Evgraf Evgrafovich playing piquet. Mamenka was still not back. He took a turn of the room, ate a pear, and without saying goodbye left once again, leaving his briefcase and umbrella in a prominent spot in the hall.

Mamma Klavdia Ivanovna. Mamenka Xenia Andreevna. A successfully transacted bit of business, a hearty lunch, the films in that house he knew, money tucked away in the bank, a few thoughts about the fate of Europe, and a possible ticket to any one of a number of evening establishments where the doorman would greet him at the entrance with a bow. That was his life. He had a right to say: 'It's me, thank God.' Once in a while it all wore a little thin, but then that didn't happen more than once in five years, after all. True, the perfected mechanism, those creatures that wore those exquisite stiff sleek boots, knew no inner conflict their entire lives, and that meant that he, Astashev, was a representative of a period of change. What could he do? We have to console ourselves with the fact that everything is relative and the individual of the transitional period is an advanced creature in comparison with Mademoiselle du Pont, who died of unrequited love, or with the sculptor Engel, who eats nothing but rabbit food. If in moments of groundless melancholy we can't turn to the people of the future (the degenerate Slavic soul lacks any real space-age energy), and if there still aren't, if they haven't thought up yet, associations for people like him, advanced people ('and there are lots of us, lots and lots of us, lots more than you think!') to march and sing in chorus, then we can turn to people from the past, who in those moments are somehow so troubling, and irritating, and essential.

The evening was cold and damp, and the city's stones and lights were frozen in the deep twilight of the streets. Oh, those boulevards, which led to the edge of the city, which he now walked along as their master, and which he at one time trod with the thought of dying in rags, poor and humiliated.

'Nothing special, gentlemen, nothing special,' he mumbled, striding with a spring in his step and already making out Engel's dark house in the distance. 'You're a bohemian,' Astashev prepared himself to say, 'and I'm a bohemian when I have to be. So it's all right to drop in on you at this late hour, isn't it?'

'Thank you for coming by. Thank you.' Engel said joyously when he recognised his visitor. He held on to his hand for a long time. 'Welcome. Won't you come in and sit a while? You look tired. Did you come on foot?'

They both walked into the studio.

'I'm very happy to see you, my dear man,' said Engel, 'although I don't have any need of you at all now. None at all.'

Astashev spoke quickly:

'You took out insurance with someone else?'

'Sort of. But not insurance. I straightened myself out. Sit down, anywhere. Relax.'

A big swarthy man in a heavily creased, dusty black jacket and grey striped trousers was still stretched out on the sofa. He wasn't sleeping, but apparently he had just woken up.

'The artist Kharin. Came in from Florence today,' said Engel. 'Mishenka, please sleep. We aren't going to bother you.'

The artist Kharin shifted around for a minute or so, found a comfortable position, and was still.

They sat down on two stools right by the window, in which both of them were reflected, and Astashev rested his puffy hands on his knees because he had nowhere else to put them.

'It came to me gradually. Maybe it's not even over yet, but the one hint has already made things much easier. Don't think that I've taken to frequenting church, confessing, taking communion, hanging up icons. No. But now I know that God is necessary. Prayer is necessary. Otherwise it can't be done.'

'My congratulations,' said Astashev. 'I have an old mamma. I must tell her about you.'

Engel wrapped his smock around himself, huddled up, and slapped his pockets, feeling for a smoke.

'I'm so grateful to you for coming by to see me. If you only knew what went on inside me after the first time! I was minding my own business and suddenly you show up – like the archangel's trumpet. Now I know that death is like passion. You can't explain it; you have to feel it. Some people live to old age and never discover that; others might grow up knowing it. So it came to me at the age of thirty-eight. *What*, you ask, came to me? That's something I can't answer. The words are all so trite – "the awareness of inevitability", "the certainty of one's own end" – and all that implies. Let me make one more comparison: "She kept on whispering: I'm yours." That's from a love song, and we don't pay attention to it any more. But if you really think it over!'

'And she, full of passion,' added Astashev. 'I heard it on a record.'

'It seems to me that here is the crux of all human wisdom – the sense of death, the idea of the end. Because you can understand everything except for that. You can accept everything except for that. These thoughts of mine nearly drove me out of this window once. But my instinct was correct. When you were here last time, though, I already knew that it's impossible without God, but I still couldn't say so. Now I'm happy.'

'From the bottom of my heart, I congratulate you. Evidently even your health has improved since then. Your colour seems much better.'

Engel smiled, his mammoth teeth seemed to make his head lean forward.

'The small hope – weighing no more than an eyelash perhaps – of not dying, of fixing something, of resolving something, of seeing someone, of running into them . . . someone dear whom you cannot recall without tears. But the main thing is being, being, carrying on in some way. Now I know what that is. For me that eyelash outweighs the universe, and even the doubts themselves seem like bliss to me in comparison with how I was living before.'

'So you still do have your doubts all the same?'

Engel squeezed his two bony hands into two dark fists and brought them up to his chest.

'Oh, not like before.'

Astashev shuffled his feet under his stool.

'I'll be going now, if you don't mind,' he said. 'I stopped by for a light, as the saying goes, and walked in on an auto-da-fé.'

'Yes!' Engel exclaimed joyfully. 'Go now! I don't need anything more from you at all.'

Astashev stood up. Still wearing his coat and carrying his bowler he walked through the studio, slowly looking around, as if reluctant to leave. On the table lay a thick earthenware platter with a shiny dark green glaze.

'A cunning thing,' said Alexei Georgievich pensively.

'Would you like me to give it to you?' Engel was already hugging the dish to his skinny chest. 'I was wanting to give you something as a remembrance all along. As a souvenir. Take this. It's not worth anything, but it's very pretty. You could put something on it.'

Astashev didn't refuse. With the platter under his arm, he walked out, having said goodbye to Engel and bowed silently to the back of the artist Kharin.

On the street he breathed freely. He had felt as though he was suffocating all evening. Only now did he realise that he had started feeling suffocated and out of sorts in the twilight of the afternoon's films, and ever since then, all day and by now well into the evening, he had been carrying around that choked feeling, that melancholy, inside him. One definitely had to arrange some kind of retreat for oneself in life. He'd been at it ten years already, and now it was time: either piquet with Vyazminitinov, or fishing, or conjugal bliss, or something else to fill up his spare time.

'I've always developed harmoniously,' he thought. 'And at forty this natural thought has occurred to me. One can't just go through life like a beast of burden: occasional women; office gossip; my lady mamenka and her cavaliers. Enough. I've been missing something, and it's been eating away at me for two days now, ever since that night with Zhenechka. She wouldn't take any money. A sweet girl. She was so frightened!'

He walked and walked, carrying his unwrapped green platter the way officials carry papers to be signed. Walking felt pleasant. The doctor had advised him to walk as much as possible to fight off the fat. This evening walking mechanically brought back his equilibrium, but he still didn't feel like going home. For the third time that day he set out for Xenia Andreevna's. It was already too late to go out, but he could sit up with her until midnight so that he would finally feel like sleeping.

He rang twice. Steps rang out in the distance, her steps, heavy but still quick; even her house slippers had French heels. She opened the door a crack.

'You? What has happened?'

'I can't sleep for some reason. Let me in. I left my umbrella here. Here's a platter for you as a present. You could put something on it.'

Dressed in brightly flowered silk pyjamas that flowed and glimmered, she led him through the dark apartment to her bedroom, sat down on the bed, and lit a cigarette.

'I was getting ready for bed. I've just got back. Imagine, that young girl (fool that I am,

I thought she was innocent!) had an *ami* and killed herself yesterday.'

He was standing over her. He looked her in the eye and pretended he didn't understand, surprising himself that he understood right away. Why? After all, it was inexplicable, mysterious. How could he have guessed that Xenia Andreevna was talking about her?

'No, she poisoned herself with gas. The owner of the cinema said that the night before some gentleman came by for her. She was living with him – that's clear. Maybe she was pregnant? Maybe he was tired of her. My God, what scoundrels you all are!'

He asked quickly: 'What gentleman? Are they looking for him?'

'No one knows who. Why look for him?'

'Was there a note?'

He didn't understand what was going on inside him. He felt liberated from a two-day nightmare: brooding, his conscience, dreams, sadness. Once again he was utterly free, absolutely tranquil, light of body and firm of soul.

'Sit here. Don't look, my hair's a mess. Anyway, to me you're not a man. I've even taken my teeth out . . . You know, her aunt got so upset that she sent for me. What, they didn't have anyone closer or something? Her mother didn't even show up all day.'

'The bitch,' said Alexei Georgievich calmly.

'It's a good thing I ran into Yuli Fyodorovich on the street. I took him along. He took care of everything. Her aunt wanted to lodge a complaint, but what was there to do if she was found in the kitchen with a pipe in her mouth, the gas pipe, that is. My hands are cold even now.'

'Calm down,' he said loudly and firmly. 'That person misled both of us. If she was so sensitive, why did she wear lipstick and nail polish and sew buttons on her dress? It's illogical, unreasonable.'

'Her lover must have left her.'

'Mamenka, what are you saying! What, no lover ever left you? If women are going to poison themselves because they've been abandoned, the human race will come to an end. You have to know how to live, how to survive: bravely, beautifully.'

'You're all scoundrels,' she repeated with affected coarseness.

He kissed both her hands, which now, without her rings, were unrecognisably old. Then he walked over to her vanity table. Since childhood he had felt a strange attraction to all items of the feminine dressing table, and now he dabbed himself with

perfume and lipstick, ran a brush through his
hair and a powder puff over his chin, sniffed
some cream, touched her scissors.

'I know people,' he said, cleaning his nails.
'Oh, how well I know them, Mamenka!
Everything is always their fault. They deserve
what they get. I could talk about it to a
Tolstoy or a Dostoevsky, but we don't have
anyone to compare with them these days. It's
not worth dirtying your hands with the ones
we do have.'

Hanging onto her headboard with both
hands and swinging her bare blue-tinged feet,
she watched him.

'In my opinion, suicide is the most unforgivable act there is.' He stuck his fingers
through the gap in his waistcoat, thrusting
out his chest. 'Something that should be
strictly prohibited. To destroy everything
that's come before! And, have you noticed,
Mamenka, it's always out of some selfish
cowardice: Oh, there's no way I can pay off
my gambling debt! Oh, he offered me neither
his heart nor his hand and took advantage of
my feminine weakness!'

He stopped and looked at himself in the
mirror. She waited for him to go on. Her
sallow face, greased for the night, her low-
slung breasts, her hair, which had recently

become copper, and her still lively, still flashing eyes, despite the bags, were perfectly motionless. All of a sudden she cracked her knuckles and said in a muffled voice:

'Alyosha, how I love you! So intelligent, so profound and elegant. I can imagine how many females you have hanging around your neck!'

For a minute he felt a searing pride in his chest, and then, when it went away, he jumped up and plumped her pillows.

'Go to bed. You're exhausted. Don't worry about the women. I don't allow them to hang. Sweet dreams.'

Lazily wrapping herself up in a shawl and yawning with her empty mouth, she saw him to the door.

So he went. Umbrella, briefcase. His soft hands swung from side to side, back and forth. His brisk legs pressed down on the stones. Through the darkness of the streets, through the gloom of the city, he walked towards the sound sleep of the Astashevs. Then, the next morning, once again – a call on the pilot in the suburbs, in the sun and the wind, wearing his freshly brushed bowler. Onward, onward, with a spring in his steady step – citizen, taxpayer, consumer (but no soldier!) – past people and over borders, carrying a flimsy passport in one pocket, a pen in the other, through the fog, through the heat, through the grey drizzle, one, two, left, right, crawling like a shadow over everything he encountered, handing out cigarettes, hinting, reminding, bowing low, leaving a trail, already a little flabby, already balding, with gold in his broadest of smiles, already breathing just a little more heavily, jiggling the pale fat of his baby cheeks as he walked, up stairs, down side streets, along thoroughfares where cars raced, over rails where trains passed, and on, past cemeteries, women, monuments, sunsets.